THE

Garry Kilworth

THE DROWNERS

Mammoth

First published in Great Britain 1991
by Methuen Children's Books Limited
Published 1992 by Mammoth
an imprint of Egmont Children's Books
Michelin House, 81 Fulham Road, London SW3 6RB

Reprinted 1993 (twice), 1995, 1998

Copyright © 1991 by Garry Kilworth

The right of Garry Kilworth to be identified as author of
this work has been asserted by him in accordance with the
Copyright, Designs and Patents Act 1998

ISBN 0 7497 1049 7

A CIP catalogue record for this title
is available from the British Library

Printed and bound in Great Britain
by Cox & Wyman Ltd, Reading, Berkshire

To Patricia and John Spiers

Chapter One

When he was nine years old Tom Timbrell was almost killed by a poem.

'Poems can be very dangerous things in the wrong hands,' his father would say, when recounting the incident. 'A person's got to be careful with things like poems.'

The way he said it, left the listener wondering whether there were two things in life that went under the name of poem. The first, a piece of verse, penned by a poet. This we all know about. The second, some sort of deadly flyaway weapon, brought back from exotic lands perhaps by a wandering soldier; a weapon with a powerful spring, which in unskilled hands was likely to go off without warning, and pierce the eye of the handler with a sharp missile.

In fact, what had happened was that young Tom had been given a verse to learn in school, and had been so absorbed by the poetry he had walked into the lock, and almost drowned. Though his father would have disapproved, Tom's head was always full of such things. John Timbrell had told his son the day after the accident that his schooling days were over, but the boy never did quite shake off his education.

His mother, Martha, often remarked that the boy couldn't help being clever, bless his heart, though she was well aware that learning poetry and such was of little use to a Master Drowner, or even a lock-keeper for that matter.

Father was more concerned with keeping his children alive.

In his winter years, John Timbrell's opinions were hardened to what he believed to be facts.

'Always treat a river with respect,' he told each of his many children, when they reached an age of understanding. 'Never take her for granted. She don't strike offen, but when she do, it's quick as an adder. River's got no concerns for age nor

1

whether you be a boy or a girl. It'll take what's there, and never a thank'ee left behind.'

The River Itchen, which flows through the Hampshire city of Winchester, is no different from any other. In the first third of the nineteenth century it was a lifesaving force, providing sustenance, but now and again needing a sacrifice.

In the dead still of winter, 1815, the river froze over. Young boys and girls strapped blocks of polished wood on their feet to go skating over its surface. The River Itchen took two at once that year, when they crashed through thin ice and sank down into the clutches of its freezing currents.

Later, in the early spring of 1824, the Itchen burst its banks and carried away three gypsy caravans on a voyage from which the inhabitants never returned.

It stole living people and returned pale corpses in their places, washing them up afterwards in the gentle ripples of some quiet backwater, as if ashamed of its flashflood tempers.

John's son Tom, when so informed of the vicious side of the Itchen's nature by his father, took note of the advice.

'I know what you'm saying, Father, and I promise to keep attention, always.'

'Good boy, for there is wicked currents down there. And cold eddies what'll suck the breath from your lungs. There's roots of trees what creep under the mud and grip your ankle, and waterweed what'll tug your arms and legs and hold you fast. Remember all that, son.'

'I will, Father.'

'Good boy, good boy, now pass me my jug of ale.'

Tom Timbrell was twelve years of age. He lived near the banks of the Itchen, in a cottage attached to a lock, not far south of Winchester. He could see the broad tower of the great cathedral where mortuary chests held the bones of ancient kings, and on a still day he could hear the sound of choirs singing special masses, that would float over the water meadows.

Whenever Tom could find time to visit Winchester, the

2

capital of Saxon England before London usurped its throne, he would run to the cathedral to stare and wonder at the medieval wall paintings and the black marble font carved with scenes from the life of St Nicholas.

One of John and Martha Timbrell's seventeen children, Tom was either ninth in line after his sister Susan, or eighth after his brother Ben. No one really knew for sure. The parents became confused when it came to the middle bunch of their brood, and before the children were able to count for themselves, their ages were jumbled and were never able to be sorted out. They did not mind that so much. They counted themselves lucky that for most of the time they were called by their right names, though a few of the infants occasionally found themselves in the wrong family order.

A rich couple might have marked the separate cots with the name and age of each infant occupant, but in the Timbrell family there were only three beds. One for father and mother and the latest baby, one for the female children and one for the male children.

In such circumstances, it was not surprising that during celebratory family gatherings, when the excitement was high and the air was full of chatter and laughter, a small child might suddenly wrinkle its brow, burst into tears, and wail, 'Who am I, Mamma? Is this my birthday party, or *Joe's*? I can't remember.' And mother would look at father with round questioning eyes, only to receive an embarrassed shrug in reply.

Nevertheless, they were a comfortable and reasonably happy family, for besides being the keeper of a lock on the Itchen, John Timbrell was the Master Drowner for all the tenant farmers on both sides of the Itchen in and around the vicinity of St Cross.

In addition to managing the main tributary where it forked into separate channels, John was responsible, as each springtime approached, for calculating which sluices should be opened, for how long, and in which order. In this way the

3

water meadows over a wide area of countryside would be flooded to a shallow depth just as the winter was drawing to a close.

Water is warmer than land in the winter. By flooding the fields the farmers were able to encourage a thaw beneath the surface and bring on the fresh spring grass some six weeks earlier than in other parts of the country. Their cattle would be feeding on the lush leas, growing fat, and be ready for market before those of less fortunate herdsmen. The dairy cows, too, would produce rich milk, butter and cheese, much sooner than would herds without the advantages of the water meadows.

One warm September evening Tom and four of his brothers went down to the Itchen for a swim. They had been pea picking in the fields and had earned an hour's leisure before the close of the day. Damselflies were skimming the surface of the water and martins came to swoop upon the clouds of midges that gathered over the shallows.

'Last one in's a rotten spud,' cried Arthur, the eldest at fourteen years, and the boys all stripped down to their skins and ran and dived into the cool green waters. They had chosen a wide bend on the river, where the flow was gentle and the bank was dripping with elderberries and long grasses.

'Whaaa! Who said it weren't cold?' cried eight-year-old Dan, but Arthur and Tim ducked him amongst the reeds for complaining. 'I still say it's mighty cold,' cried the victim, once he had surfaced again, his hair dripping weeds as well as water.

Tom said, 'You've been saying how hot you felt all day. Now it's cold? Make up your mind, Dan.'

Daniel stood up, reached down and scooped up a lump of soft river mud. 'You'll be sorry you spoke them words, brother Tom, I'm almost sure you will,' and he hurled the sludge at his older brother's head, laughing at the same time.

Tom ducked, the mud went over his left shoulder, and he heard it slap on the bank behind him. Then he saw Dan's expression change, and the faces of his other brothers all of a sudden turned serious. He looked around and up, to see what

4

they were staring at, and his eyes met those of a lean broad-faced man, who had been quietly standing on the grassy verge.

'Which one of you little curs threw that?' snarled the man, pointing at his pitted boot, where the missile had splattered.

The voice was harsh and aggressive. The face like granite, boulder-hard. Tom stared at the man, seeing in his features a violence which was worrying to a young boy. The fingers that gripped a gnarled and polished hickory stick were scarred as if from many brawls. They looked strong enough to crack a cow's ribs. Though the day was warm the man wore rough thick clothes, the bottoms of the trousers tied with baling string. His body had a fibrous look to it, as if there were no spare fat, only just enough tough muscle to spread across his thick bones.

The eyes, though, were the most worrying of all. They were narrow and pale blue, carrying a coldness that chilled the beholder.

'Which one of you monkeys, I say?' growled the man.

Arthur cried, 'We bain't monkeys, nor curs. We be John Timbrell, the Master Drowner's, sons and Dan didn't mean no harm, sir. He were just larkin'.'

The man with the stick raised his left fist.

'I'll give him just larking, if he comes out here.'

Daniel very wisely showed no inclination to leave the water to be given something by the man on the bank.

The man wiped his foot on a tuft of grass and then regarded the boys from beneath his black brows. His penetrating eyes outstared each of them in turn. Each time he forced the eyes of his watchers away, he whacked the instep of his boot with his hickory, as if marking up a victory.

'Timbrell's sons, eh?' he said at length. 'Aye, Timbrell's sons. Well, you tell your father from me that Wesley Wickerman is here. He won't've heard on me, but that's to his disadvantage. If he'd been round Tilbury Docklands, he would'a heard on me. I banged a few heads there that won't be forgot. If he'd been in the streets of East London, he would'a heard on me. I crushed a few ribs there too.

'I got some advice for that father of yourn. You tell him Sir Francis got hisself a new man, one what knows the law from the law and don't care either way. He gets in my way I'll crack his skull like an egg ...' the stick was raised as if proof of his threat '... for Wesley Wickerman steps aside for no man, Master Drowners especially. You got them words, you monkeys?'

The boys nodded.

'Don't go forgetting them.'

With that the man who called himself Wesley Wickerman, the new man of the great landowner to the north of the county, Sir Francis Alderton, strode off along the river bank.

Their swim spoiled, the boys scrambled out of the water on to the bank, and dressed quickly, not even waiting to let themselves dry. They plastered their hair flat with their fingers, put on their caps, and set off for home.

Chapter Two

Like the others, Tom had in mind the fact that Sir Francis hated the local drowners and tenant farmers, who were not mortgaged to him but to the Winchester banks. The aristocrat wanted them out of business. The reason he disliked them was, of course, because they beat his cattle to the markets every spring and took the best prices for their beef and their dairy produce, before he was able to get his own produce in front of the buyers.

Sir Francis Alderton was a strange man, hardly in evidence on his estates, for he spent most of his time in London. He hired managers to look after his land, which he visited when the need arose, and he never ceased to rail at any of the tenant farmers if he caught them on the road. He would drive past them in his carriage and, leaning out of the window, would abuse them with his sharp tongue until he could no longer be heard. For a gentleman, he was hardly a gentleman. He was intensely jealous of the drowners and their method of flooding the water meadows, which kept him a permanent second in all cattle dealings in the county.

The five brothers walked along the dykes to their cottage, not saying anything to each other. They were lost in their own fearful thoughts. The darkness was coming in, soft and black, across the fields, down the funnel of the river. Birds were finding roosts for the night and particular trees, that were favourites of the starlings, were covered with feathered blobs, chattering and hollering for all they were worth.

As they neared the house, Arthur said, 'He were a rum one, that 'un. I didn't like him, not one jot. What shall we tell Father?'

'We must tell him what happened,' said Tim, 'mustn't we?'

Tom spoke then.

'I say we don't speak a word of it. You know what Father's like, when someone calls him out. He'll go looking for this Wesley Wickerman to give him a piece of his mind, and that's what the man wants, for sure. Father's over sixty years old now, and not strong. He's strong enough to get through winters, but not to stand toe to toe with a younger man, a man like this street fighter, who looks as cruel and mean as a mad bull.

'I say we don't speak a word of it.'

Benjamin agreed with his brother Tom and, eventually, the others all nodded their heads before going through the door of the cottage.

The tenant farmers beside the Itchen had been using their method of drowning the water meadows for centuries, long before Sir Francis had arrived on the earth. However, the vast patchwork meadows and networks of canals, irrigation ditches, channels, dykes and sluice gates, had grown steadily more complex as time passed, and the flooding was a complicated, delicate operation.

Too much water and the fields became sodden, useless: too little and a late frost would freeze them over.

John Timbrell was the Master Drowner, on whom the other drowners relied. He knew the signs of the weather, the rotation of winter-summer crops, the absorbency of the pastureland, as well as the complexities of the sluices.

Tom was his apprentice.

The reason John Timbrell had chosen Tom, out of all his children, to follow in his footsteps, was because the boy was not as strong as some. Though not sickly, Tom was small in stature, with narrow limbs. A Master Drowner required brains, not brawn, of which Tom had ample. His brothers on the other hand, besides helping with the lock, were built for working the land. They hired themselves out as farmhands, ditchers, faggers, and any other work which required muscle and stamina.

Tom had been his father's apprentice since he was nine years of age, and had proved a quick learner.

When the boys entered the cottage, the rest of the family were round the massive table which John Timbrell had fashioned from the frame of a discarded brewer's dray. The four wheels had been sawn, top and bottom, so that their edges were level with the lip of the table and flush with the floor below, thus forming legs. Some of the children had to sit with their legs through the spokes.

The pole to which traces had been attached had, of course, been removed, and was used as a washing post by Martha Timbrell, the children's mother.

There was cheese and bread in plenty on the table. A jug of cider for John and the older boys was at the east end, while water and milk containers stood at the west end. There was plum jam to be had, and some of the girls were spreading it thickly on their hunks of cheese as the boys walked through the door.

Sally, somewhere in the middle of the ages, said, 'Oh, the boys have been swimming. Them all wet.'

'You mind yourself,' said Arthur, 'we've been working in the fields all day long.'

'And what have we been doing then,' sniffed Sally, 'but your dirty washing, and tendin' the vegetable patch, and feeding the pigs and chickens, an' ...'

'All right, all right,' grumbled Arthur, taking off his cap and slapping his thigh with it. 'Next time *you* can go swimming and we'll stay home and do some chores, how about that?' Which speech stunned the listeners into silence, for Arthur had never been known to volunteer his services around the house before that night.

Martha Timbrell asked, 'Are you feeling well, son?'

Arthur took his place at the great rectangular table, with Tom on one side and Tim on the other. Their seat consisted of a long thick plank of wood resting on two barrels, one at each corner of the table. There was a similar seat on the other side,

where the girls sat. Father sat down one end, flanked by the
two eldest boys, both wearing the wispy beards of almost-men,
and Mother distant but opposite him, her two eldest daughters
at her elbows.

'As well as anyone here,' said Arthur, 'thank'ee, Mother, for
asking.'

'Well!' replied the stout mother of seventeen children, as if
she had truly seen the eighth wonder of the world. 'Well, I
never did.'

Then she sat down with a thump on a beech chair that had
been specially made to take up the spread of her enormous
bottom.

Tom ate his tea in silence. He was very worried about this
new man of Sir Francis, and guessed that Wesley Wickerman
had been sent for on purpose, probably to harass the local
tenant farmers. Tom could foresee trouble coming, without
having to look very far ahead. Wickerman's fists could kill, he
had no doubt of that, and when a man died in street fighting,
the law considered it as much his fault as that of the opponent
that struck the mortal blow.

Wesley Wickerman had said that John Timbrell would not
know him. That was probably true, but *Tom* had heard the
name from a travelling diddicoy. The pedlar had told him
about a strong man born in the village of Hursley, five miles
southwest of Winchester. This fellow had, before he was
twenty, walked to the London docklands, and there was hired
by shipping companies to break up social clubs which were
gradually forming into trade unions. Wickerman's method
was to go into public houses and challenge club organisers to
fist fights out in the street, there to pummel the victim to
insensibility.

It was not difficult for men like Wickerman to provoke a
fight, pretend to turn it into a sporting event for the benefit of
the watchers, and then batter their inexperienced victim with
deadly precision. He knew where to hit, where to cause the
most damage. Hard blows beneath the heart would put paid to

a man frail in that area, and if that did not work, the kidneys, or the temple.

Tom was afraid for his father. John Timbrell had a dangerous enemy in Sir Francis, though Tom had not previously thought the aristocrat would stoop to such tactics as using hired killers to eliminate the opposition.

After supper, Tom took over from a sister at managing the lock gates. As the night came in it became quiet on the river. A barge passed through, lamps swinging fore and aft. This longboat was pulled by a great shire horse, a gentle giant with masses of hair round its thick ankles. Once it was gone, Tom opened the wooden sluices to keep the water flowing during the night. As he worked the winches he could hear the bargeman calling, 'Giddap there, booy, cum on, cum on, giddyup there ...' into the night sky.

The craft was the last of the day's river traffic. Blackness was upon the waters, the reeds had melted into shadow, the trees were barely discernible in the starlight. Over and beyond the water meadows was the glow of Winchester, from the lamps which lit its quaint passages, its crooked ways, its cloister and green, and winding streets – all of which the bronze statue of King Alfred, holed and green with corrosion, had guarded for nearly a thousand years.

Tom wished the statue of the great Saxon warrior to life, so that he could protect his people from the tyranny of men like Sir Francis Alderton. But bronze remained bronze in the still evening, and Tom went sadly to the bed he shared with his brothers.

Chapter Three

The tenant farmers and their drowners were gathered in Jack Riley's old barn. It was evening and the moon shone through the cracks in the roof, marking the dirt floor with slivers of gold. There was straw strewn over the ground in patches, adding further to the moon's efforts to fool the avaricious.

Jack Riley, otherwise known as Whoffer, due to a habit in his idle youth of asking, 'What for?', whenever he was asked to do some chore, stood up and raised his hands. He was now closing on seventy, but still the question snapped out occasionally, when he was feeling belligerent and crusty of a cold morning.

In action against Napoleon, Whoffer had several parts of his body missing. One arm, a leg and part of his remaining hand had all been left in Belgium, when a cannon Whoffer was loading exploded. If anyone suggested that Whoffer was only half a man, he would call them a liar.

'Oi be just as full-whole as the next man, 'n a bit more besides,' he would say. 'Oi be just spread about more, that's all. Oi be a man o' two countries. Half on me in Belgie, half on me in Hampshire.'

'And what's the bit more?' he would be asked.

He would rap his last good three knuckles on his leg and arm.

'Good, solid Hampshire wood,' he would say. 'Live when it were attached to me, and kep' alive by this 'ere heart 'o mine, pumpin' sap an' blood. Sap an' blood. That's what's a-runnin' through these arteries. Roots in Hampshire earth. Part man, part tree, an' settled across a continent. Ye won't find more of a man than Jack Riley, anywheres.'

Certainly none of his spirit had been left on the battlefields near the village of Waterloo. It was, if anything, much more intense, for having been concentrated in a smaller amount of flesh. He was a fiery, feisty old man, who would stick his chin out at the Devil and ask him what for.

Whoffer opened the meeting of the farmers and their hands, with a loud, 'Roight! We're all 'ere, 'septin Jones, an' ee bain't coming, so we'll get roight on. Alex Blunden as got summat to say.'

With that Whoffer sat down on a bale of straw, folded his arms, and stared at his legs. One of them was made of crack willow, as was his left arm from the elbow down. Children used to follow him around, asking if they could borrow his arm to use as a cricket bat.

Alex Blunden, like most of the men present, was a farmer and a drowner. He had a face the colour of beetroot, especially at times like now, when he was called upon to do some public speaking. One of his fingers played nervously with a piece of string threaded through the buttonhole of his jacket, which served to keep the garment closed.

'You all know what happened to me t'other morn, as I were coursin' hare with me old dog Rupert. I were met on Pastor's Lea by that there Wesley Wickerman, Sir Francis's man. He tole me I were trespassin' on his master's land. I tole him not to be so daft, since everyone knew Pastor's Lea were common land, and a cat or a king could walk there if they pleased.

'With that he struck me down with his fist ...' Alex Blunden displayed a bruise on his cheekbone, just below the left eye. 'He tole me not to be so damned impudent. Then he walked off on me, before I could get back on my feet. I went straight to the manor, o' course, to complain to Sir Francis and get some satisfaction for my hurt, but he weren't there at the time. I left a message with his butler, to pass on, but the only reply I got back were from Wickerman. He sent a boy to the inn, where I were supping a mug 'o rough to soothe the pain, and the lad said that Wickerman would knock my head off if I was to go near the big house again ...'

'That sounds bad,' said John Timbrell. 'Sounds to me like

this Wickerman's trying to cause you to fight him. A man would be daft indeed to do that if he weren't sure of winning, wouldn't he? So we go to assume this London man is a bit of a rough 'un ...'

'Rough 'un?' interjected Blunden. 'He's as mean as a weasel with a maggot in its ear.'

John Timbrell nodded, a little irritated at the interruption. He liked to get things off his chest before others started putting their spokes in.

'What we can be sure of then,' John said, 'is that Sir Francis has put him here of a purpose, to put the frights into us. Sir Francis don't like us, that we know, and no doubt will stoop to all sorts of tricks to get us to sell our properties and leave. He'd buy 'em all right, quick as that, you can be sure. We got to stand up to this Wickerman and not back down all the time.'

'Back down?' yelled Alex Blunden. 'I hardly had a chance to get me mouth open, afore I was knocked silly. Nex' time ...'

At that moment, the barn door swung open and two local constables stepped inside. They both had their night sticks in their hands. Behind them stood the very man the farmers had been discussing for the past twenty minutes: Wesley Wickerman.

One of the constables spoke.

'I'm told there's an unlawful gathering being held in this barn, for purposes of conspiracy.'

Whoffer gasped. 'Conspiracy? 'Gin what?'

'A plot against Lord Alderton, so I've been told.'

John Timbrell said, 'And who told you that whopper? Him, I suppose?' and pointed to Wesley Wickerman, who was standing quietly behind the two officers, gently slapping the palm of his left hand with his hickory.

The constable looked embarrassed.

'It don't matter who our informant might be, the fact is that the law is being broken here. Citizens may not gather for the purpose of conspiring 'gainst any other man, let alone a peer of the realm.'

'Treason, that's what it is,' interrupted Wickerman stepping forward, his eyes sweeping the barn. 'A plot against the crown. Why, *His Majesty* might be the next victim of these rogues and scoundrels, if we let them get away with it.'

John Timbrell cried, 'There's no plots being hatched here, not against no one!'

Wickerman's eyes narrowed.

'Do you deny that the name of Sir Francis was used here tonight? Do you deny that animosity was spoke against this name? Well, out with it, man? Do you deny you slandered the good name of myself, Wesley Wickerman, without so much as a by your leave, or a thank you, sir?' he roared. 'Do you, man? Why, I ought to crack your skull where you stand ... but of course, these officers of the law can take care of the likes of you, and your nest of rats. Constable?'

The policeman in question cleared his throat.

'This meeting must be broke up, forthwith, or some of you will find yourselves under arrest. Come on now, off home with you.'

John Timbrell was almost speechless, but he blurted, 'Well, I never ... of all the underhand.' He gathered his self composure. 'This is a perfectly legal meeting of farmers ...'

'Like thieves in the night, under cover of darkness,' snarled Wickerman.

'We *works* durin' the day,' yelled Whoffer, 'not loike some. Ye call me a thief, ye young puffball? Oi'll knock the wind out of ye, so oi will. Oi moight be mostly willer tree, but oi'll put a bit o' wood atween those eyes o' yourn.'

Wesley Wickerman glared at the old man, and John hastily continued what he had been about to say, before Whoffer hopped across the room on his willow-leg and swung his willow-arm at the pugnacious face of his accuser.

'Perfectly legal. We might have mentioned Sir Francis. It's well known he's jealous of our method of drowning the fields in winter and beating him to market. We might have mentioned a certain Wesley Wickerman, and as how he struck another man, Alex Blunden, without being provoked and seemingly out of sheer nastiness of character. But there is no plot against either Sir Francis, or this Wickerman.'

Wickerman said, 'If this is a meeting of farmers, what's a lock-keeper doing here?'

'I'm the Master Drowner, for the water meadows. It's obvious why I'm here.'

'Obvious? Damned suspicious, I say.'

Some of the farmers had begun to drift towards the door at this point, no doubt thinking that there was little point in continuing the meeting while the constables were urging them to leave and while Wickerman continued to argue with anyone who tried to speak. Whoffer Riley told John that he had best go home, and Alex Blunden took the Master Drowner by the arm, whispering, 'We'm better go home together, John, for protection like. Anyways, I got somethin' to speak to you about.'

The two men left together, with John Timbrell still seething. Once outside though, the Master Drowner had to concentrate on finding his way across the fields, for the moon had gone and the lanterns they carried provided poor light, especially for men of their age with failing vision.

On the way, Alex Blunden spoke seriously to John, about his own son Jem Blunden. The men said good night to each other at the crossroads, with Alex Blunden adding, 'Think on what I've asked you, John.'

When John reached the cottage, and entered, he found Martha sewing by the light of a lamp.

'You'll damage them eyes, sewin' in such dimness,' he remarked, his mind really on other things.

'Hummph,' Martha exclaimed, 'they'm not damaged yet and I've been sewing such all my life. Anyways, children have got to be clothed, and I've enough of them to keep me busy till I turn up my toes, thank heavens.'

John muttered something in agreement, then went through to the boys' bedroom, where he woke Tom.

16

'What is it, Father?' Tom said, sleepily, as bodies slumbered beside him, some stirring in their sleep.

John whispered, 'Son, you know I want you to take over as Master Drowner, when I die ... no, no, it's got to be spoke of ... anyways, Alex Blunden has spoke to me about his son Jem. Says he thinks I should have a second apprentice, alongside you, in case summat happens to one of you. It's all right while I'm alive and kicking, but leavin' the knowledge of the drowning in one head is a dangerous thing to do. I think I agree with him, but I want to know your feelings on it.'

Tom was quiet for a moment. He was thinking that, of all the boys he knew, Jem Blunden was the one lad he went out of his way to avoid. The pair of them had never got on well, since a scrap in their younger years, when the older Jem left Tom with a bloody nose and had received a swollen ear in exchange. They never spoke to each other now and when Tom saw Jem from way off he took another path to his destination, knowing that any face to face confrontation would only lead to conflict. Consequently they had not been within fifty metres of each other since Tom was ten years of age. Tom believed his adversary had grown so strong over the years, and mean and full of hate, that he was now invincible. Tom quaked at the thought that he was going to have to surmount this barrier that had found its way between them.

'Father,' Tom said in measured tones, 'Jem Blunden and me don't see eye to eye, but if he's the one you have chose to do this, then I'll have to put up with it.'

'Good boy,' whispered John Timbrell, 'now you get back to sleep.'

'Like the rest of us is tryin' to do,' muttered a sleepy voice from the middle of the bodies on the great bed.

'Who said that?' growled John, his eyes sweeping the prone and supine forms in the half light, but there was safety in numbers and the culprit kept his identity secret.

Once his father had left the bedroom, Tom lay awake staring at the ceiling. His heart was pounding a little with the thought that he was going to have to meet his enemy face to face once again. When he thought about it, it was probably the best thing that could have happened, for the pair of them *had* to get on together now. It was just that, well, the first meeting would be difficult. Tom was not looking forward to that meeting.

However, the summer months were long, and such a meeting would not take place before winter came upon them. There was time to get used to the idea. In the meantime, Arthur's foot was in his mouth and Tim had rolled over on to his arm and given him pins and needles. It was time to assert his bed-territory rights over his brothers, which he did by tickling or pinching, to clear his own small space on the straw-filled mattress.

Chapter Four

Jem Blunden was driving the hay wagon from Morgan's Pasture to the hayrick in his father's barn. There was much on the boy's mind and his freckled face beneath the thick hair (cropped unevenly by his sister Nellie with a pair of sheep shears) wore a look of deep concentration mingled with anger. He flicked the worn leather reins in an attempt to urge the cob to greater speeds than its normal plodding pace, but these efforts were quite unsuccessful. Polly knew the way, kept her own clock, and the journey could have been made with less fuss by her alone, and no one up on the cart.

Jem was short and stocky, with squared shoulders and heavy-looking legs. His eyes were set wide and saved from appearing too small by a constant look of enquiry. He was normally slow to anger, but once he was there, his face flamed and his body shook and violent action followed. During his three years at school (quite enough in his opinion) he was only in trouble for fighting twice, but both times were serious and resulted in a leathering from the schoolmaster, endorsed by his father.

It might have surprised some to find Jem in his work clothes, which consisted mainly of his sister Mary's hand-me-down dress, except that at least a third of the boys around Winchester wore their older sister's shifts. If you came from a poor family and had older sisters instead of brothers, you wore the cast-offs from the girls. That was the way of things and no one thought it strange or would have considered teasing Jem because he wore a female garment.

He also wore his uncle's tattered floppy hat and smoked a clay pipe. At thirteen, Jem was doing a man's work and was, therefore, a man to everyone but his mother.

Not many people teased Jem in any case. He did not invite

such behaviour. He was at that precise moment in the day, a time drawing on towards evening with a redness stealing through the thin clouds, grumbling to himself.

'C'mon, you old snail,' he muttered at Polly. Then, 'I don't know why I should've been chose to be a Master Drowner. Me with only three years' schoolin', but Dad says it's so and therefore it must be's. That Tom Timbrell, he must be laughin', just itchin' for us to get together so's he can lord it over me, with my slow way of thinking ...'

Like Tom, Jem was going through agonies over the prospect of coming face to face with his old enemy, successfully avoided until now. Tom's prowess as a boy with a quick mind and sharp wit was so worrying to Jem that in his own head he had built Tom into nothing short of a genius. He knew he could knock young Tom into next week when it came to fisticuffs, but he also knew from experience that Tom, bloody nosed and bruised, would always have enough breath and fire left for a parting retort. A sharp rejoinder that would deeply wound his assailant.

Although he would never admit it, Jem was far more vulnerable to being hurt by words, and he was dreading the meeting with Tom. Still, that would not be until much later in the year and maybe by then his own brain might have expanded and he would have grown cleverer. Jem didn't give much hope for it, but he was not beyond clutching at straws.

In the meantime, his main ire was directed towards one Mr Wesley Wickerman, who had struck his father and knocked him down before Alex Blunden could defend himself. Jem was incensed at this cowardly action, and had determined to get even with this man Wickerman.

'Just let him wait, Polly,' said Jem, flicking the reins and causing the mare's ear to twitch in irritation. 'Just let him come across me and see what's in store for him. I'll show Mr Wickerman what's what, that's no lie.'

Polly disregarded the youth's chatter and plodded steadily

on down the lane with its lengthening shadows and its hedges covered in twittering balls of feather and bits of fluff. She had her mind on the lush grass which fringed the ditch, or failing that, the hay in the back of the cart. Horses have very singular channels of thought.

Jem and Polly came to a turn in the lane which was flanked by dark woodlands. The trees along this dirt road reached over on either side to form an archway, worn to shape by the wagons that passed beneath it and chipped away the new shoots that threatened to extend themselves over the passageway. Inside the long archway it was already night, the trees having earlier sent the daylight on its way.

Jem was always uneasy in this tunnel of foliage, simply because of the silence and gloom, but there were distractions which helped him allay this feeling. Foxes sometimes crossed his path, moving like messengers between animal conspirators, plotting to overthrow mankind. There were badgers in there, too, with their rolling gait, appearing like sailors who have just disembarked and have not yet got their land legs. Weasels, stoats, rabbits, martens. The mammal wildlife was rich and varied.

Polly, on the other hand, didn't give a thin straw, either for darkness or for foxes and their kind. The wagon wheels creaked their way steadily to the end of the tunnel, the cart swaying in the ruts that had been made in wet weather and had failed to harden in the sunless passageway.

By the time the pair of them emerged into the world again, the redness in the sky had darkened to a deep purple and long lanes of shadow were stretched across the land.

Suddenly, Jem strained his eyes against the failing light, to perceive a figure coming along the lane towards the cart. As it came closer, Jem could see it was a man in rough tweeds, carrying a stick in one hand and a lantern in the other. The man's stride was confident and there was great strength in the legs. Jem could see a power behind that walk which no doubt extended throughout the man's whole physique. Though the man's stature was not of alarming proportions there was something very forceful in his bearing.

'I can't be certain sure, Polly, but I'm betting that will be Mr Wesley Wickerman, delivered up right into my hands,' whispered Jem. 'He's got that rawboned look my dad spoke of, and he walks like he owns the whole kingdom. It must be he ...'

The cart moved forward a little, for they were on a slight incline now and Polly was tired at the end of a hard day's work. She would not stop, nor falter in her stride, but her pace dropped to about half its original speed. Wesley Wickerman, albeit on foot, was moving much faster towards the cart, than it was towards him.

'C'mon Polly,' urged Jem, his breathing tight and his voice even tighter, 'let's be having you.' Beside Jem's seat was a heavy club made of wych elm. He used it to clout rabbits when chasing them through the corn stubble of a harvest time. His right hand reached across and his fingers closed round the weapon.

Wesley Wickerman approached the cart and slowed his walk a little, since there was not much room either side between the wheels and the ditch. The man drew up alongside Jem in the gloaming, and glanced up at the youth.

For a second, their eyes locked.

Then Wickerman growled, 'Well, what are you staring at, boy?'

Jem looked down into those iron blue eyes and saw something which brought a flush to his features and a shaking to his hands. He let go of the club and gripped the reins until his knuckles turned white.

'Nothing, sir,' he said.

'Then be on your way,' said Wickerman, with a contemptuous wave of his stick. Then the man was past, striding out towards the woodland arch, the heels of his boots flicking up mud from the damp strip where the edge of the ditch met the road.

Jem was quiet for a while, allowing the momentum of the

cart's swaying movement to rock his body from side to side. When he finally spoke, his voice sounded cracked.

'That were Wesley Wickerman,' said Jem to Polly, in a strained tone, 'and for all my chuntering I didn't do a blessed thing.'

Though Polly couldn't see it, and wouldn't have understood if she could, the tears were silently streaming down Jem's cheeks.

The wagon creaked on in the twilight and Polly's wheezing was the only other sound in the world.

Chapter Five

Wickerman was wondering why the boy had looked at him so closely, as if he had seen his dead grandfather or something. The locals, Wickerman had long since decided, were a dense lot: turnip heads, every one of them. They gawped and gaped like fools at the most ordinary of sights. They might be primitive savages for all they knew of the world.

The opening to the tunnel of leaves drew closer, looking like a black mouth large enough to swallow a man. Wickerman stopped and took time to light his lamp. The darkness was around him like coal dust now. He always had a little difficulty in breathing in the dark. Though he suspected the cause was not entirely scientific it was nevertheless so. He experienced a tightening in his chest and his breaths quickened. It seemed he could never quite get enough oxygen to satisfy him while he was in the darkness.

'The cold night airs, no doubt,' he told himself on many an occasion. 'The damp humours of the evening. They probably affect many a man, if I did but know it.'

He failed to question why, once the lantern was sending out its comforting rays and illuminating his path, his breathing became much easier. Coach lamps do not warm the atmosphere of the night, no matter how hot the flame behind their glass.

Wickerman entered the long tunnel, feeling the softness beneath his feet of a road carpeted by damp leaves and kept eternally in shade. He could no longer hear his own footsteps and the silence seemed to move against him like an assassin. He paused just inside the entrance, to look back at the fading sky, which appeared much lighter from inside the womb of the wood.

'Another day ...' he said, and the tone was almost wistful.

He turned again and strode out along the passageway, the swinging lamp causing shadows to jump back and forth across his path.

'The boy ...' he mused. 'He gave me a look, that was certain. He's one of the drowners' brats, I'll be bound.' Wickerman suddenly gave a little chuckle, which the wood quickly muffled. 'Scared the tyke, though. Frightened the little puppy out of his wits. Face as white as a sheet on my staring him full in the eye. Then when I spoke, why he went redder than a maid caught showing ankle ...' He chuckled again, and again the sound was deadened by the surrounding tangle of branches and briars.

Wickerman paused for a moment and listened, thinking he could hear a coach or wagon coming down the tunnel, but there was no light. The sound was probably that of an underground brook, or the wind in the boughs above his head.

He shrugged and moved on, quickening his pace a little, turning his thoughts to other things.

That morning Sir Francis had come down from London to see how his new man was progressing, and Wickerman was pleased to report that he had the farmers and drowners worried.

'I think I've got 'em on the run, my lord,' he said, standing cap in hand, uncomfortably aware that he had an expensive Persian rug beneath the soles of his boots. He was not used to opulence, and he hardly knew where to put his feet, or place his hands. Everything around him was crystal or silver, brocade or finely-woven silk, and for a man used to leaning on a pinewood bar, with a brass rail for his foot, the situation did not instil him with confidence.

'Don't call me 'my lord',' said Sir Francis, absently, 'I'm only a baronet. 'Sir' will do perfectly well ...'

Wickerman screwed his cap in his hands, not in servitude or anything remotely close to it, but to prevent himself uttering something he would regret later.

25

'Yes – sir,' he said.

He was not used to rich surroundings, but neither was he used to being patronised, and he did not like it. Baronets, lords, they were all one to him. A bunch of high narrow noses. He liked the pay he was getting, but he was not going to grovel for it.

Sir Francis was no fool however. Shrewd, ruthless and cunning, but not stupid. He prided himself on being able to judge a man's temper to a fine hairspring. To him men were like time pieces: they ran according to the quality of their parts. When a cog or escapement was worn, the clockwork was out of time. Outward signs of wear, like that which he witnessed before him, told him the person before him was running too fast.

He nodded at the cap.

'You'll tear that thing in half if you're not careful, man. What's the matter? Don't you like being taken to task?'

'You're giving me good wages, sir, but I don't like to be spoke down to, not for an instant. I'm sorry for it, but there it is.'

Sir Francis looked amused, and twiddled with his *pince-nez*.

'No, you're not sorry at all, are you? Well, we'll try not to get on each other's nerves, since I hear good reports of your work. Keep it up, Wickerman. It will take time, but I want those people out of business eventually. I don't hold their mortgages, more's the pity. The banks do, and I have no control over the banks. Try not to kill anyone. Death is so very final and threats are so much more effective, particularly when vague. If they don't know what you're going to do to them, they'll spend their waking hours wondering and worrying over the precise nature of your next move. Well done. It will be a slow business, I've no doubt, but we'll get there.'

'Yes, sir. Thank you, sir.'

Sir Francis said, quizzically, 'Nothing much frightens you, does it, Wickerman? Not lords or ladies, not tough, hardened farm labourers? You're an iron man, through and through, am I right?'

'I was brought to manhood on the streets of the east end, sir. I ain't afraid of no man, nor his brother.'

'Good, good. You'll have a glass of something with me, before you go?'

Wickerman shifted his feet on the silk carpet.

'I'd rather be about my business, sir, no offence.'

Sir Francis raised a practised eyebrow.

'Is that a put-down?'

'No, sir, I'm just not used to drinking ale without sawdust under my boots.'

'Ah, the surroundings. I understand. Well, perhaps we might go down to the inn together – in my coach of course, I cannot go so far as to *walk*, I'm afraid – it might be well to be seen together in public just once? It will give you some status, increase your authority. What do you say?'

'The inn would be fine, it's just ...' Wickerman waved his cap at the ancestral portraits on the wall, with the aquiline nostrils.

'Of course, as I remarked.'

So, the meeting had gone well, all in all. Sir Francis was no silly fop, that was for sure. He knew how to treat a hired man, and he had a keen eye for upsets in character. At the inn, he had drunk ale, not wine, which had impressed Wickerman.

There was a sharp *crack* in the woods to his right, and Wickerman started out of his reverie. He swung his lamp round causing the thickets to dance around him.

'Who's there?' he called, gripping his hickory tightly and brandishing it like a cudgel. 'Who's out there? Step forward and have your head knocked off!'

There was a deep silence following this request, during which Wickerman thought he could hear shallow breathing.

'Hello!' he cried.

Still no answer.

Wickerman waited for a few more moments, before

hurrying on down the long dark tunnel. The trees and undergrowth jumped and darted around him, causing him to look this way and that, and occasionally to miss his footing. He saw with relief that the end of the corridor of foliage was getting quite close, when suddenly a white disembodied face came out of the wood, into the lamplight for an instant, flying directly at him. The features were demonic, with large staring eyes.

'Aghhhhh!' he cried, and dropping the lantern he thrashed his arms around his head.

The shape flapped for a few moments in the passageway before disappearing into the darkness of the wood. On the ground the lamp was on its side and it spluttered and went out, leaving him in complete darkness. A nameless panic leapt to his throat. Wickerman felt as if he were choking and had only one thought: escape from the dungeon of darkness.

He ran blindly forward, straight into a thicket, and claws caught his clothing, scratched at his face. He lashed out with his fist, striking at things around him, and kicked with his boots, and flailed with his stick. His left hand became sticky with blood as he struck solid objects, though he felt no pain.

He then fell back and rolled on the damp leaves, fortunately touching the lantern with his arm as he did so. He felt around him with shaking fingers, found the lamp, and managed to light it again. Evil shadowy wraiths instantly flew off into the darkness. The twisted blackthorns, which had been moving towards him, sprang back again into their rightful places.

Wickerman's breath was coming out in short, sharp gasps, which he fought to control. Once on his feet again, he hurried towards the opening at the end of the tunnel and out into the starlit night. There he stood, his sweat cooling, and stared about him for a while.

When he had regained his composure, he began walking again, muttering to himself, 'It wasn't nothing but an owl, I'm almost sure of that. Nothing but an owl. There's no such thing as ... as ...' but he couldn't even bring himself to say the word, and his feet crunched with a comforting rhythm on the hard road from the inn without further interruption. Wesley Wickerman was afraid of no *man*, nor his brother, that much at least was certain.

Chapter Six

It was early morning, the mists were winding over the water meadows, between the legs of the cattle. Moorhens were complaining of lost positions on the river. John Timbrell had just been giving Tom a tour of the sluices, and asking the boy questions to test his knowledge of the drowning by posing various situations and asking Tom how he would deal with them. John was, in the main, quite impressed with the answers. Tom seemed to have obtained a good feel for the work, and had satisfied his father on most accounts.

'Remember,' said John, 'to test for the depth of the last frost, and allow for soak-away.'

'That I will, Father.'

'Good, good. Now I understand your mother is sending you off to Twyford, to your cousins there?'

'Arthur and Mary and me are going down by rowboat.'

'Well, I send my best regards to all at Twyford. Tell them that, Tom.'

'Yes, Father.'

They went back to the cottage by the lock. There were beards of algae attached to the wooden joins in the sluice gates: they trailed long and green in the flowing waters of the Itchen's offshoots. The river was faster than normal today, there having been some rain near its source on the Hampshire Downs. The water running over the edge of the weir, rarely heard by the inhabitants of the cottage, was like liquid glass falling from the grassed terrace.

Inside the cottage, Martha had laid the brewer's dray with breakfast and some of the children were already tucking into a meal of green fish, a pot of milk pottage, and several herring pies. There was the usual animated discussion in progress amongst the boys, about who had stolen most of the bedclothes and whose territory had been usurped during the night.

The girls, of course, were above such pettiness. They had more important things on their minds like the fair that had arrived on the green, complete with a tent for dancing. They talked about it, without openly asking their parents if they could attend, hoping to instil the idea subliminally.

Tom and his brother and sister set off downriver for the village of Twyford just before nine o'clock in the morning. Mary was in charge, being the eldest at sixteen years, but Arthur flexed his own desire for authority occasionally, being a strong-willed youth. He and his sister argued over almost everything and Tom, in trying to ignore them, found himself communing with the ducks and keeping a sharp eye out for wildlife.

Arthur was rowing, but since they were going with the flow of the river, he did not need to work very hard.

'Mary, you'm sitting in the wrong place,' grumbled Arthur. 'You'm upsetting the balance of the craft.'

'Oh, the balance of the craft, is it? Well, I'm sure I don't want to do that, Arthur, but I think I know more about boats than you do, that's certain.'

'Do not!'

'Do so!'

Thus it went on, pausing only for Mary, who was coming of age, to find a miraculously swift and sunny smile from under her frown for a young fisherman on the bank.

'I'm tellin' Mother of you,' said Arthur, straining the hemp rowlocks. 'You'm flirting.'

Mary stuck out her tongue.

Tom, used to his brothers and sisters quarrelling, continued studying the river. There were banks of rushes on either side, with the occasional clump of yellow flag and reedmace. Coots and moorhens slipped into this river foliage when the boat approached them. Like most river children, Tom was fairly knowledgeable regarding the wildlife on the water. He knew, for instance, that the coot has a white blob on its forehead while that of a moorhen is red. He knew the difference between the amber and the shiny-glass snails. He could recognise the call of a bunting, and had caught many a water vole in his time.

He was rewarded by a kingfisher diving for whirligig beetles and excitedly pointed to the colourful bird.

'Kingfisher!' he cried.

'Seen it,' sniffed Mary.

'So what?' said Arthur.

Tom gave up on them.

Mary took over the rowing a little later on, and the two boys got out fishing lines, to trail them in the water after the boat. Arthur was lucky and managed to land two roach before they came to a wide shallow stretch of river. Being unfamiliar with this part of the waterway they managed to get the boat stuck, and had to get out and drag it over the gravel bed before continuing their journey.

Just before they reached the spot where they were to take the path to Twyford, they came across a landing stage full of young men and women dressed in fine picnic clothes. There was a party in progress and people were unpacking hampers, and talking in high voices. One young man shouted something to the trio in the boat, waved his hat, and then let out a laugh, but the wind was in the wrong direction and neither Tom nor the others understood what had been said.

Mary stopped rowing as they swept by the end of the landing stage, and said enviously, 'Look at them dresses. All white and billowy. And them hats with all the ribbons. I wish I had one of them ...'

'Well, you ain't,' said Arthur cruelly, 'so it's no good wishing, is it?'

She took up the oars again and skimmed them across the top of the water, splashing her brother.

'Hey!' cried Arthur.

'Serve you right,' muttered Mary.

They reached the Twyford path soon after, and carried the

things their mother had packed for their cousins to a cottage not far from the river. The house was built principally of a kind of kealy earth – firm and strong and more durable than soft stone or poor brick – drawn over with lime-mortar. Cruck-framed with rough uncouth oak forks, it was covered in cowdung once a year which, when dried, served as fuel for the fire.

Their cousins greeted them with enthusiasm and a natural truce was silently agreed between Mary and Arthur while in the presence of their relations.

Tom went off with Albert, a boy of his own age, who showed him how to make french arrows fly. You simply took the arrow, fletched with a goose feather, and wrapped a piece of knotted string once around the shaft. You ran the string taut to the point of the arrow and used it like a sling to launch the missile. It flew through the air as if it had been shot from a bow.

Tom was delighted with the new toy.

'We do competitions,' said Albert, 'to see who can sling their arrow furthest off.'

Mary and Arthur were singularly uninterested when Tom returned to the cottage to show them the wonderful invention. Nevertheless, he knew his younger brothers would be enthralled with the idea, and carefully wrapped the arrow in a piece of muslin, as if it were a delicate cheese.

The three of them said their goodbyes and went back to their boat, to make the journey home. A strong wind had sprung up, channelled by the river banks, and it took one person on each oar to battle with both the weather and the current. They were going upstream now and this made for hard work.

Arthur and Mary were rowing as they approached the party on the landing stage. They heard the revelry from a long way off. Someone was playing a fiddle and stamping his foot, while others were dancing on the rickety jetty. When they turned the bend in the river, they could see the group, their clothes flying about them, careless of the high wind. Hats could be seen in the water, drifting downstream and an upturned parasol went rapidly by the rowboat, spinning in the swirling eddies.

Mary sighed, wistfully.

'Lot of foolishness,' muttered Arthur, getting in before Mary could follow up on the sighs. Once they had rounded the bend, the gale increased in ferocity. The high wind seemed to do nothing but excite the revellers, for they shrieked with laughter when a wicker stool went tumbling over the edge of the landing stage.

Then something happened: one of those unusual phenomena for which people are never prepared.

Instantly, the mood had changed. There was a scream, followed by shouts of alarm. The music stopped abruptly. A white and flimsy figure, like a giant blossom, was floating up and out from the jetty. A woman, a small and fragile person with delicate bones, had been standing on the edge of the high landing stage when the wind came up beneath her stiff skirts and filled them. She was suddenly lifted up and carried out a metre over the water.

Then her skirts collapsed and she plunged into the racing currents of the river.

One young man would have immediately jumped in after her, but was restrained by his companions. There was confusion amongst the party. Then on seeing the rowboat, the men began shouting hoarsely to Tom, Mary and Arthur, to grasp the women as she floated by them.

Arthur stayed calm.

'Here, Tom, take the oar while I get to the bows, so's I can catch hold of her.'

'Right, Arthur,' cried Tom, quickly changing places with him.

Mary and Tom steered the boat out into the current, to be in the drowning woman's path. Looking over his shoulder, Tom could see the terror in her pale face, as she was swept along, her head slipping under the surface every now and then. Her dark hair was streaming out behind her, as if it were chasing her head, trying to keep up with it.

34

Just as Arthur reached out, to clutch her dress, the woman went under, disappearing beneath the braided ripples. Her eyes were still open, the fear in them naked.

A loud groan went out from the crowd on the landing stage.

'I missed her,' cried Arthur. 'Turn the boat!'

Mary lifted her oar automatically, and Tom swung the craft round, to point it down the river. Then Tom saw the ghost-like veils of the woman's dress running just under the surface, near to his hand.

'Here she is,' he shouted, and without another thought he dived into the river, reaching for the material. As he went down, the dress receded from him, eluding his grasp.

Up in the boat, Arthur was now in a panic. He searched the water around for signs of the pair and let out a huge yell when he saw the woman bob to the surface, just a metre away from the rowing boat. With Mary holding his legs, he leaned out and grasped her by her hair, pulling her close to the craft. Then with his sister's help, though the boat was skimming crazily sideways, he hauled her over the gunwales to safety. She was choking and sobbing, but still alive, water spilling from between her lips. A faint cheer went up from the jetty, but the pair in the boat were still in agonies of distress. They searched the waters for signs of their younger brother.

'Where's Tom?' cried Mary. 'Oh, where's our Tom?'

Chapter Seven

By the time Arthur and Mary got back to the landing stage, some of the men had at least managed to launch their own skiff. They searched the banks for a mile downriver, calling for Tom, prodding the reedbeds hoping he had crawled out alive but was perhaps too weak to answer.

When two hours had gone by they began throwing out lines with weights in the hope of finding Tom's body. Mary and Arthur, still frantic, kept saying that Tom couldn't be dead, he was a good swimmer, he knew how to survive in the water, despite the currents. They went up and down with their rowboat, shouting themselves hoarse.

Dusk arrived, the men lit lamps, but took the two youngsters aside and told them gently that there was no longer any hope for their brother. They were sorry for it, *dreadfully* sorry, but Tom was a hero who had laid down his life for another. The search would go on of course, for as long as Arthur and Mary wanted it to, but the shame of it was the river had taken a victim, though everyone prayed otherwise: it would be a miracle if Tom were still alive.

'What are we going to tell our mum and dad?' whispered Mary. 'What about them?'

She had stopped crying now, having shed many tears over the course of the evening. Arthur, wrapped in a blanket, was just staring at the ground, shivering every once in a while. He wanted to comfort his sister, but had no words left. He needed comfort himself.

There was a young man present, brother to the beau of the lady who had fallen in the river: the same man that had to be stopped from following her into the swollen waters. His name was James Halliwell, the second son of a genteel family.

He spoke to the distressed pair.

'Our gratitude for what you have done today, I have to say, is boundless. We are all very much in your debt. Your young brother's courage has put us to shame. He has humbled all of us. If you will permit me, I shall come with you to your home, which I understand is the lock-keeper's cottage further up the river. I think it would be better for you, and your parents, if I explained what has happened here this evening.'

'Thank you, sir,' said Mary. 'We should like that.'

Arthur nodded, silently.

Halliwell took them in his family coach, travelling through the darkness, despite the danger of pot-holes in the road. They arrived at the cottage very late. Lamps were in evidence and men were standing in small groups around the lock.

Halliwell stepped down from the coach.

'I should like to speak to the lock-keeper,' he said.

John Timbrell stepped forward, lantern in hand, but he was abrupt with the stranger.

'If it's business of some sort, I can't talk to you now, sir. Three of my children is overdue, and should have been here hours since. We're waitin' on them this very minute ...'

The young man drew a deep breath and said, 'I know of your children, Mr Timbrell. I have some grave news. Are you steady, or do you wish to go inside the house?'

John Timbrell lifted the lamp to James Halliwell's face and looked into his eyes. He did not like what he saw there. The apprehension he had felt for several hours now turned to cold horror in his breast. Nevertheless, he was anxious to hear what this serious young man had to say.

'Steady. I be steady, sir.'

For his part the man with the bad news noticed that the lock-keeper was completely drained of colour. Halliwell placed a hand lightly on John Timbrell's elbow.

'There's been an accident, on the river. Your daughter Mary, and your son Arthur, are safe. They're with me here, in the carriage ...'

'And Tom?' cried John Timbrell. 'What about my Tom?'

37

'I'm afraid he's missing. We have men searching the river at this very moment, but there's little hope. Would you like to sit down, sir?'

The lock-keeper was swaying, but he pulled himself upright with effort. He stared straight into the eyes of the man who stood before him.

'Tom's dead,' he said in a flat voice. 'It's clear in your face.'

'We believe he's drowned. He went under and never surfaced. There was a clear view of the river from where we stood. Of course, there is a chance that he came up further downstream, but our search revealed nothing, and he would have been under the water for a long time – too long, I'm afraid.'

James Halliwell paused to let this sink in, before continuing.

'I'm dreadfully sorry. He dived into the river to save a lady, my brother's fiancée, who was in terrible difficulties. The lady was rescued by Mary and Arthur, but your son Tom was somehow held by the waters. I am most profoundly sorry.'

John Timbrell nodded brokenly. He went to the carriage window and looked in on Arthur and Mary, and at the other empty seats, as if to make sure Tom was really gone. They stared back at their father, knowing how he was feeling, wanting to say something to ease his pain, but having no words.

John Timbrell turned to address Halliwell. He spoke to him in quivering accents, though it was obvious he was trying to keep his broken spirit from shattering completely.

'Would you like some refreshments, sir? Before your return journey?'

Halliwell, aware that a mother had to be told of the death, shook his head.

'Thank you, but no. I have to be getting back – immediately in fact. Let me leave you my card ...' he pressed his calling card into the large fat hand of the lock-keeper noting that the man was shaking '... and should you ever need any help, do not hesitate to contact me. My family are in your family's debt, sir, and we shall be only too happy to repay you in any way we can. You are too full of grief at the moment to think straight, I am sure. I shall leave you to your sorrow and call again at a later date.'

John Timbrell nodded dumbly.

The children, assisted by Halliwell, climbed down from the coach and walked towards the cottage. Their father followed right behind them, aware that he had to be the one to tell Martha. Mary and Arthur had already been through a great deal and Arthur seemed to be in shock.

James Halliwell climbed inside his coach, but not before he had spoken quietly to one or two of the men, who were now drifting off into the night. The coach then left.

The last man to depart from the scene was Alex Blunden. He stared at the silent cottage for some time. Then when the sounds of grief penetrated the night air, he shook his head sadly and began walking towards Winchester where his farm lay.

It was a grey day, with much rain.

The church where the funeral took place was an austere countryman's place of worship, out along a lonely lane with no other buildings for two miles on either side. The nearest structure was a tithe barn out beyond the water meadows. There were yews outside the drystone wall that marked the churchyard boundaries, which gave shelter or threw shade on the headstones, depending on the weather.

They held a memorial service without a body, which was never found. James Halliwell, Peter Halliwell, and his fiancée Edwina Caudieron, all attended. Miss Caudieron was almost fully recovered from her ordeal, and wept softly when the memorial stone, paid for by the Halliwells, was set in place in the churchyard. *In Memory of Thomas Timbrell*, read the inscription, *who selflessly gave his life that another might live. Greater love hath no man than this.*

Arthur had Tom's french arrow, which he buried at the foot

of the stone, but that was all of Tom that went into the Hampshire earth. The waters of the Itchen had the rest of him. Some possessive willow root was probably wrapped lovingly around his small body, keeping it from the world above, holding his last home a secret from the sky.

Wesley Wickerman passed by the church as the service was in progress and nodded coldly to one or two faces. If he was satisfied by this turn of events, he did not show it, but left the family to mourn their dead without revealing his feelings.

In the weeks following the funeral, John Timbrell went into decline. Tom was not the first child he had lost, but he was the first to go over the age of two years. The man began wasting away, hardly eating, rarely speaking. His hair had turned completely white almost overnight, and his once large red face developed loose grey flesh and became deeply lined.

Towards the end of autumn, his spirits seemed to pick up a little, and he began talking about the drowning of the fields. He chose another of his children, as apprentice Master Drowner, and told Alex Blunden that he had not forgotten about his son Jem.

Then one cold December evening he put on his greatcoat, scarf and hat, and informed Martha that he was going to the inn. It was not a thing John Timbrell did often, but there were occasions when he professed a desire for a jug of ale with his fellows, and took a walk to The Royal Oak Inn.

When John did not return before midnight Martha became alarmed and sent her two eldest out looking for him.

The young men found their father stretched out hard and cold in the alley that gently separated the dark-beamed Godbegot House from The Royal Oak Inn. He was frozen through to his heart. There were no marks on his body, which might have indicated a struggle with an unknown assailant. Nor had he fallen down drunk and helpless, victim to the icy easterly that blew across the open meadows, for he had died on his way *to* the inn, and had never tasted a drop of the ale he had set out to drink.

John Timbrell had not been past Tom's memorial stone since the funeral, and it seemed that when his tired eyes had fallen on the stone for the first time, his heart had just given up on him in despair.

This second tragedy, so close to the first, stunned the whole community. They rallied round the Timbrells, offering help in many forms. Martha, hardly over Tom's death, seemed to find a strength from deep within her. She realised at once that their situation was desperate. John Timbrell had been the lock-keeper for the Itchen's subchannel, and the cottage was tied to the work. If one of her sons did not go to the authorities in Winchester and claim the job as his own they would be homeless.

The two eldest boys set out a day later, hoping that the authorities would appoint one of them in their father's former position. They returned in the evening to give their mother the worst possible news. They had been too late. Someone else had applied for the position just a few hours earlier, and on the recommendation of Sir Francis Alderton had been successful in that application.

The new lock-keeper's name was Wesley Wickerman.

Chapter Eight

Martha Timbrell once more gathered together her consider-
able inner reserves of strength, and sent Mary off to Twyford,
to the home of the Halliwell family. There Mary spoke with
James Halliwell, who in turn rode many miles on horseback to
visit Sir Francis Alderton. It was a bitterly cold day,
threatening rain, and James Halliwell was quite frozen
through when he arrived at the manor house.

The sixty-year-old Sir Francis received him in the library,
where there was no fire in evidence.

'What can I do for you, Halliwell?'

The two men were known to each other, Sir Francis being an
adversary of James Halliwell's father in the political arena.

'I'm on a mission of mercy,' smiled James Halliwell, hoping
his contempt for the man before him did not show through too
blatantly. 'I understand your man Wickerman has been
appointed the new keeper of the main lock on the River
Itchen?'

'Your information is correct.'

'Is it necessary that this Wickerman should hold two
positions? I'm told he's your gamekeeper, or estate manager,
something of that sort, in which case you will have already
provided him with accommodation.'

'Possibly,' snapped Sir Francis, looking pointedly at his fob
watch. 'Get to the nub, if you please. I'm late for an
appointment in London.'

James Halliwell stifled a retort, hardly able to keep the
coldness out of his stare as he regarded the other man.

'I'm sure I don't wish to keep you from your parliamentary
business, but the family of the former lock-keeper, a John
Timbrell, has no other home to go to. I have persuaded myself
that you were not aware of this state of affairs, and hope you

will now see your way to asking Wickerman to withdraw from the post of lock-keeper. The work has been in the family's hands for generations – as long as the lock has been in existence – and any one of the older sons or daughters is competent to do the job. It would be a great kindness on your part to ensure their reinstatement.'

Sir Francis Alderton, who had never been in the kindness business, smiled thinly.

'Would it now? And what's your interest in this?'

James Halliwell stiffened at the tone used by the baronet.

'If I needed a reason to help an old Hampshire family in distress, it would be that certain of the Timbrell children saved the life of my brother's fiancée, now his wife. One of the rescuers, a twelve-year-old boy, drowned in the act ...'

'Yes, I heard about that. The young fool jumped in the river, while it was in full flood. Well, I admire his spunk, but it's hardly my fault he drowned himself, is it?'

Halliwell shook his head.

'I wasn't suggesting for a moment that blame lay anywhere. I merely wish to request that your man withdraw himself from the position of lock-keeper.'

'I'm afraid that's impossible.'

The two men stood a metre apart, staring at each other for a few moments before Sir Francis Alderton turned away to look out of the window of his driveway, lined recently with poplar trees by the famous landscape gardener, Capability Brown.

'Now if you'll excuse me, Halliwell, I see my coach is ready.'

'You won't do it then?'

Sir Francis whirled to face him again.

'Haven't I just said so? Not in a thousand years. I need my man installed amongst those scoundrels down the river. A spy in their midst, worrying them, causing them to look over their shoulders the whole time. Now they've lost their Master Drowner and his assistant, almost at a stroke, I have them where I want them for the first time in fifty years. I intend to follow up my advantage and see that damned water-meadow system of theirs fall into disuse.'

James Halliwell said very slowly, 'You're a vindictive greedy bitter old man ...'

The elderly aristocrat started backwards, then raised his bony fist as if to strike the young man before him.

'You young jackanapes! Insult me? In my own home? Get out. Get out.'

'Gladly.' James Halliwell turned on his heel and left the house. He did not breathe freely until he and his horse were two miles down the road from the estate, such was his anger.

James rode through pastureland lightly covered in hoar frost: a cold still kingdom where only hares had left their padprints on the meadows. His mount's breath came out in large plumes then crystallised within seconds. His own chest felt as if a cooper had circled it with an iron barrel hoop and was tightening it slowly. The skies above him were like marble, swirling with mottled blacks and greys.

He rested his horse in the stables of The Green Man Inn some few miles away from the lock-keeper's house. While the grey was being rubbed down and watered, James washed away the grime of the road. He then found the parlour and took a bench not too far from the fire, ordering refreshments from the burly landlord at the same time.

Thus far the day had been cold and dry, but while James was partaking of a dish of beef and bread, a storm announced its arrival with several claps of thunder. Soon, near-frozen rain was drumming down on the roof of the inn, rattling the slates and windowpanes. James, now thoroughly warmed through, decided to stay where he was, in front of the roaring log fire, until the fury of the inclement weather abated.

While he was lingering over some local biscuits and ale, a man entered the parlour enveloped in a thick cape from which ran rivulets of water. He stood in the doorway for a moment, staring into the gloom of the dark-beamed room with its low ceiling, and his eyes settled on James, remaining there for an

44

ill-mannered length of time. James returned the stare, knowing he was looking into the eyes of Wesley Wickerman.

Finally, James said, 'Have you seen enough, sir? Or shall I turn and present you my back, so that you have a complete image?'

'Mr James Halliwell?' growled the other.

'If it is of any business of yours.'

'My name is Wesley Wickerman and I understand from my master that you're an interfering young upstart ...'

Within a second James was on his feet and standing directly in front of Wickerman. The hired man made a motion, but his arms were hampered by the heavy cloak he wore. James reached down and gripped Wickerman's wrist through the cloth. Wickerman, the stronger of the two, wrenched his arm away. He smiled infuriatingly into the young man's face.

The landlord stepped from behind his barrels and pushed some startled patrons aside in order to get to the two men before fighting started.

'Outside, if you please, sirs. I won't have my establishment turned into a rough house.'

The rain was hitting the roof like lead shot when suddenly, as if God had given a signal, it stopped. In the silence that followed both men ignored the landlord's request.

James said in unfaltering measured tones, 'You may be able to bully some people, Mr Wickerman, but you will find yourself outmatched with me. I will not resort to street fighting, for I have neither the skill nor the strength for such activity. As you see, I am a slight man, not fashioned for brute force. However, nature did see fit to provide me with one talent. There are those who decline to use fists or cudgels in favour of mightier weapons. Weapons that can be held easily in one hand. Weapons that can wound from a distance.'

Wesley Wickerman stepped back and looked aggrieved. He appealed to the landlord and the men at the bar.

'Did you hear that? He's talking about pistols. He threatened me with my life!'

45

The landlord scratched his head. He knew of Wesley Wickerman and he was not sympathetic to the man's methods of obtaining what he wanted. There was talk that he was turning the Timbrell family out of their ancestral home by the River Itchen.

'I heared the gentleman say some folk was good with sporting weapons, but I never heared no threat as such. I think that's what you meant, weren't it, sir? That there are them who could hit a pheasant on the wing?'

'Right between the eyes,' answered James, not removing his own from those of Wesley Wickerman.

The hired man cried, 'People don't hunt game birds with pistols ...'

'Some do,' snapped James. 'I know a man who finds any gun with a longer barrel makes hitting the target much too easy. He believes there's little sport with such weapons. He likes a challenge.'

Wesley Wickerman nodded slowly.

'I see how the wind lies, and with you, landlord. I won't forget you, neither ...'

The landlord, no slight figure like James Halliwell, but a broad-chested man with thick, muscled arms, stepped forward and jutted out his massive chin.

'I hope you won't, Mr Wickerman, because before ι is gentleman lets some air into that fat head of yourn, I shall have took great pleasure in cracking a few of your ribs.'

'See about *that*,' snarled Wickerman, and turned on his heel, stepping back out into the rain.

James heaved a sigh of relief.

The landlord said to him, 'Bad lot, that one. Good job you have some skill with firearms, sir. I hear he's free with his fists and don't care who he uses 'em on.'

'Skill with firearms? I don't even own a gun,' said James. 'I would have immense difficulty in hitting one of these four walls if I fired from a standing position in the middle of the room.'

46

'What?'

'It's my brother who is the crackshot with the pistol. The mighty weapon *I* was talking about, that can wound from afar, is the pen. My own talents lie in the direction of a man of letters – I, my dear landlord, am a poet – I could have threatened to denounce the man with a vicious sonnet, or a rather damning elegy, of course, but I somehow think that would not have impressed him half as much.'

The landlord stared for a moment, and then burst out laughing.

'By God, you've got some gumption, sir. He would have broken you in two.'

James gave him a weak smile.

'I'm very much afraid you're right.'

When the rain stopped, James continued his journey to the Timbrells'. There in the cosy room of the cottage, he gave the bad news to Martha Timbrell and her children, but added, 'Don't despair. I have some friends in Norfolk who will find a place for you on one of the canals there. I know you would prefer to stay in Hampshire – here is where your friends and relatives are – but failing that you will not go hungry. Would you like to go to Norfolk, or does the prospect of moving so far away fill you with apprehension?'

Martha wiped her hands on her apron.

'Sir, there's enough of us in our family to provide our own friends and relatives, and after what's gone on around here, what with the river taking Tom, and then my John getting took by the cold, well, I'd as soon move to a place where the memories can start afresh, if you know what I mean.'

'I think I do, Mrs Timbrell. I think I do.'

'The eldest boys will be looking for wives of their own soon, and it's best we move, if we're a-going to, before that happens. Dragging a young lass away from her home county at a tender age would not be fair to my way of thinking. Better they should find wives when they get to where we're going.'

'A sound philosophy. I'll arrange the move as soon as I can.

Please don't worry about expenses. I'll see to all that.'

'I don't like to be beholden to anyone, Mr Halliwell, but I have to think of my youngsters, and if it *has* to be, then I'm glad it's you. You're the kindest man I've ever known, setting aside my late husband John.'

'Mrs Timbrell,' James said slowly, 'my kindness is no match for that which your son showed towards a complete stranger, in giving up his life for hers.'

'You can't go all your days repaying one deed, sir, which much as I loved my Tom, was probably carried out on the spur, without thinking ...'

'Oh, yes I can, Mrs Timbrell, and I intend to. Whether Tom paused for thought or not, is irrelevant. In fact the speed at which he acted shows that his parents instilled within him a lack of selfishness which most men and women spend a lifetime attempting to achieve. I doubt I would have done what Tom did.'

Martha Timbrell smiled.

'I understand you tried, sir, but were stopped by your brother.'

'True, but then Edwina was no stranger to me.'

Martha said slowly, 'It's always struck me as strange, if you don't mind me saying so, that it was you who tried to jump in after the lady, and not your brother, the one who married her.'

James smiled wryly.

'Therein lies a secret, which you may guess, Mrs Timbrell, but which should never go beyond the two of us.'

'You was in love with her, wasn't you, sir?'

'Past tense, Mrs Timbrell. *Was.* Now she is my brother's wife, and I love her like a sister. She did not return my affection, you know, which is not surprising because I never revealed mine.' His distant expression suddenly broke into a smile. 'I'm a poet, Mrs Timbrell. Poets are always falling in love, especially with unobtainable ladies. We need to suffer, you see, and if life is too easy for us, if bread enough is on the table and wine fills the cup, then we seek out spiritual,

48

emotional suffering, in order to agonise over our verses. You see me, pale and wan, lean from suffering unrequited love, but my poetry, Mrs Timbrell – it soars!'

Martha Timbrell shook her head.

'You make light of it, but *I* know,' she said. 'And you still haven't said why you take such an interest in us all, the drowners included.'

James stared at her for a few moments before replying.

'Do you really need a reason to help people in trouble, Mrs Timbrell? Before young Tom sacrificed himself, I knew nothing of your family, nor of the troubles of your friends. I am a Christian man, my family is wealthy, and I have relatively few problems in my life. My father wished me to become a clergyman, but I have no skills in that direction. I could never be a parish priest, and I have no time for those younger sons who become vicars simply to hang a hat on themselves, while they remain as guests of the aristocracy – a token clergyman in the household of a duke or some such.

'What I can do, now that I have been made aware of the fact, is to try to assist these people if they require my help. They are my neighbours after all.'

As he rode away from the lock-keeper's cottage, James Halliwell encountered a youth, standing and staring wistfully down into the icy waters of the Itchen.

'Hello,' he said to the boy, 'are you one of the Timbrells? I don't remember seeing you before, but there are so many.'

The boy looked up at the man on the horse.

'No, sir. My name be Jem Blunden.'

'A friend of Tom's perhaps? I saw the way you looked at the river, as if it had taken something from you.'

'Not so much a friend, as an enemy, you might say. We had our differences, me and Tom. But oh …'

'Oh, what?' asked James after a moment of silence.

Jem turned his soulful eyes on the man.

'Oh, I wisht he were here now, I really do. I think he's gone and drowned because of me, you see. We was supposed to be put together, for the apprenticeship of Master Drowner, but he were much cleverer than me, and I were afraid he'd make me look a fool, so I wisht he were dead. And now he is, and it's probably my fault, for asking for it.'

'You hated Tom?'

'I never *hated* him, sir. I were feared of him, of his quick mind.'

'Then you must not torture yourself, young man. Tom did not drown because of something you, in your confused state, asked of nature. Prayers for the well-being of others very rarely receive a reply. Prayers requesting that harm befall others are *never* answered. Tom drowned because that was the fate the world had devised for him, not because anyone wished it to be so.'

'You really think so, sir?' asked Jem.

'I'm certain of it.'

James Halliwell continued his journey south.

Jem stood and watched the tall slim man, sitting high in the saddle of the grey, and felt a great sense of relief flood through him. Mr Halliwell had said it was not Jem's fault, that it was all because of the nature of the world, and he had no need to torture himself any further.

'He's a good man, that Mr Halliwell,' said Jem to himself, 'even if he is gentry.'

Chapter Nine

Martha and her family moved to Norfolk two days after Christmas, and a hard going they had of it. The world had turned to chilled bone, the roads were unyielding and resulted in sore bottoms and cricked backs. Their furniture, minus the great brewer's-dray table which had to remain behind, was taken in an old hay wain, which followed behind the covered wagon James Halliwell's father had borrowed from a tenant farmer. James had wanted to hire coaches for the whole family, but Martha put her foot down.

'There's too many of us, sir, and we'm not used to such luxury anyways. One farm wagon will do us proud, so long as it has a top to it to keep out the worst of the weather.'

Even so, the back of the wagon was very crowded, which helped the bodies inside to keep each other warm. The little ones mostly remained in the middle of the group, snuggled on horsehair mattresses, while the rest of the family moved around them in the manner of winter bees, taking turns on the cold fringe of the group, then warming up again when they changed places with the inner circle.

The journey of 210 miles, from Winchester to Coltishall village in Norfolk, took four days, travelling on average about eight hours per day. They were exhausted on arrival, but Martha sent word back to James Halliwell that they had been received with kindness and all was well. The family were to manage the lock there.

The local people, she said, were difficult to understand due to the fact that on the flatlands the frequent storms and tempests caused everyone to shout above the noise of the wind – even when it was not there – and this distorted their speech, but they were generous enough and spared no pains in helping the family settle. All manner of folk had come to see them,

51

including several tanners, fellmongers, curriers, ropers, malsters, lime burners and coopers, since the Timbrells were a curiosity having come from a foreign place, so to speak.

The Timbrells had found a new home.

Wesley Wickerman moved into the lock-keeper's cottage and immediately brought down a young man from Oxford to manage the working of the gates. Wickerman had neither the knowledge nor the interest to raise and lower wooden dams, and he and his master considered his time was better spent doing things other than siphoning river water.

The important thing being that he was now installed in the heart of the drowning country. Not that there was a great deal to do on the lock in winter anyway, but just the same he preferred to have his days clear.

The great dray table he turned into his own bed.

January saw a heavy fall of snow, which transformed the land into a soft peaceful-looking fairytale place. The woods through which Jem Blunden walked were muffled in cotton wool and he loved the quietness of his own footfalls. While he was out hunting rabbits for the pot, he caught an ermine which bit his finger and made it swell, yellow and blue-black.

Whoffer Riley lanced it for him with a knife that had been passed through a candle flame. The white-haired old man told him that if he had had a sensible piece of crack willow for a hand, instead of flesh and blood, the ermine would have gone home with a mouthful of splinters. Whoffer applied a muslin poultice smeared with soap and placed it over the wound to draw out the remaining poison.

February came in screaming with gales, which shook the snow-covered trees to stark black skeletons once again. Jem's mother made his father a new pair of trousers. The old pair were passed down to Jem, who was considered grown enough to fit them, thus enabling the youth to cast off his older sister's shift, which went down in turn to his younger brother.

52

The time came which everyone was dreading. The fields were ready for the drowning, and the men got together under Whoffer Riley, to talk about how it was to be done.

'Alex Blunden,' said one, 'weren't your son Jem suppose to be a-learnin' the work of the Master Drowner?'

'Never got the chance,' replied Alex. 'Old Timbrell went afore we could get Jem under him. We'm just going to have to manage as best we can. We'm all drowners here. I'm certain we can calculate what's to be done, if we put our heads together.'

So they did their best. They went on a tour of the fields, looked at the height of the river, stared at cloud columns of cumulonimbus and wisps of cirrocumulus until their eyes were sore, tested the wind with wet fingers for strength and direction, dug into the turf to gauge the depth of the frost, and did all those things they had seen the Master Drowner do when he was alive.

When they felt the time was ready, they began to open the sluices and let the water flow into the various meadows. There it found its multitude of levels, seeping over tiers from one field to another, sneaking through ditches and channels to leas and pastures, until the drowners considered there was water enough over the land.

It was a complete disaster.

Some meadows had too much water and remained flooded way beyond the time when the cattle should have been feeding on the grass beneath. Some of them had too little water and the surface remained frozen, thus defeating the object of the drowning. Only two small meadows were covered correctly, the water warming the land beneath, thus encouraging lush early grass for the cows. But two fields fed only a fraction of the cattle and the rest remained as lean as the herds owned by Sir Francis Alderton.

By the time they had fattened, the baronet already had his own cattle in the markets. He was, of course, delighted. If anything his cattle were slightly superior to those of the farmers of Itchen, since being wealthy his winter feed was of better quality and substance, and the herds started off at a slight advantage before being put out to graze. In the market place, his cheese, milk and other dairy products sold faster and for higher prices, leaving the farmers bereft of their usual advantage.

The farmers came out of it poorly, were hard pushed to make the mortgage payments on their farms to the bank. A second year like this one would ruin them completely. They were desperate to discover the secrets of the Master Drowner and wrote to Martha Timbrell asking her to tell them anything, anything that would help them.

Martha eventually replied that, much as she would have liked to have aided the drowners, there was nothing she could tell them.

Jem Blunden, in his new second-hand pants, was filling out to be a physically strong youth at least a head taller than his father. He was incensed by the presence of Wesley Wickerman at the lock-keeper's house, and used to glare at the whitewashed cottage every time he passed it, on foot or by wagon.

Once spring was over, Jem went out into the fields to try to fathom something from the vast network of sluices, dams, dykes, ditches, channels and terraces that made up the water meadows. He felt there must be some key to it all, that once you found the secret everything would fall into place and you would know exactly what to do the next season.

One day, when the dust of the summer was high, and the river ran smoothly, winding through the fields, Jem was sitting with his head in his hands and contemplating a hole in one of the dykes. If he had not come along at that point in time it was possible that the river would have breached the dyke and they would have had a flood on the land.

Jem was busy wondering whether or not to blame Wesley Wickerman for the hole, which he had now repaired with rocks and earth. It was possible that Sir Francis's man was not satisfied with beating the farmers to the spring markets, but wanted to damage them further. Then again, a burrowing animal might have been responsible. It was hard to tell.

While he was thus thoughtfully engaged, a girl appeared, walking along the top of the dyke.

When the girl, about fifteen years of age and dressed in a colourful costume, reached where Jem was standing she paused and looked down on him.

'Hello,' she said, 'your face is all fussed up.'

'I'm thinkin',' replied Jem, absently, then coming to his senses, added indignantly, 'what's it to you?'

'Nothing,' replied the girl, 'but it looks like hard work.'

'Harder than forking wet hay,' replied Jem, 'but look, what're you doing here? This is private land, see. Not just anyone can walk though, nice as they please.'

The girl was not put out and smiled at him.

'I'm up here on the dyke. River don't belong to anybody, does it? I can walk here if I like.'

Jem knitted his brows.

'I s'pose so. You a gypsy, are you?'

'We call ourselves "travellers".'

Gypsies were not liked by the local residents. There were all sorts of stories surrounding the coming and going of gypsies, most of them myths concerning their disregard of private belongings and property. It was true that they poached, mostly rabbits, pheasants and partridges, but then so did several of the local people. Poaching was a way of life, when you lived off the land.

There were those gypsies that stole chickens and ducks of course, but you will find thieves in any society. One gypsy who steals does not represent the whole itinerant group, any more than if your own neighbour kills his wife it makes you a murderer too. Yet they still got lumped together, by the villagers and townspeople, as 'thieving tinkers', if they were in the area when something went missing. If a child was lost, for any reason, the gypsies were blamed for taking it, though they had more than enough of their own little mouths to feed, without deliberately looking for more. Children they did not need.

There was a certain amount of jealousy involved as well. The gypsies were experts at recognising good horse flesh, and bred their own quadrupeds to sell in the markets. The farmers around Winchester, like the farmers around any town or city, considered themselves to be the last word when it came to horses. If a gypsy bought a bargain from under their noses, or sold them what appeared to be a frisky pony which later judgement revealed was a broken-down nag, they were quietly furious. They said nothing at the time, for who wishes to be thought a horse-trading fool, but when the opportunity arose they were quick to damn the presence of gypsies.

Jem stared at the black-haired girl and thought that she was pretty in a foxish way. Her eyes were bright and she was lean, and fluid in her movements, though he thought she could do with more plumpness in her cheeks.

'Travellers you may be,' said Jem, 'but you're still gypsies, eh? I mean, if that's what folks call you, that's what you be.'

'That's what *you* people call us, but you don't name God's creatures. He does that himself. If you called a stoat a weasel, that wouldn't make it a weasel, it's still a stoat, isn't it?'

Jem blinked at this confusing sentence, but decided to let it go.

'Anyway, what're you doing up there?' he asked. 'Where's your caravans?'

The girl pointed a slim finger at a curl of smoke beyond Dappler's Wood.

'We're on the common, that's where we are, and we'll leave when we please,' she said. 'I'm out here looking for my lurcher ...'

Lurcher? That sounded to Jem like some sort of monster, a shambling half-alive creature that went round strangling honest folk in their beds. *Lurcher*. Perhaps she had some sort of guardian, a beast that followed her faithfully around, ready to attack anyone who maligned his charge?

56

'There she is,' she cried, pointing again, this time to a spot not far away from where Jem stood.

The youth jumped back, alarmed, and spun round to see a dog coming towards them. It was carrying something between its narrow jaws. The dog was of medium size and looked like a cross between a whippet and a terrier – a lean fast dog with small sharp eyes – and it could run like the wind.

It flashed past Jem, leapt on to the dyke, and dropped whatever had been in its mouth at the feet of the gypsy girl.

Jem saw that it was a hare.

The girl picked it up and put it in a small flour sack she had been carrying tucked into her waistband.

'Did he catch that?' asked Jem.

'That's what dogs are for, aren't they?' she smiled.

Jem thought of his own dog Grip, who was a cross between a border collie and an English sheepdog. Grip couldn't catch his own tail, if directed towards it. Jem had longed for Grip to run down rabbits, or partridges, let alone hares. He was impressed and envious.

'What's his name?' he asked.

'*Her* name is Meg,' said the girl. '*My* name is Bess. What's yours?'

'Jem. It's short for Jeremy.'

'A gem is a precious stone,' she said. 'I shall call you ... Sapphire.'

'You'll call me Jem, if you call me anything at all,' he growled. 'Sapphire sounds like some fancy gypsy lady's name.' He was glad he had shed his sister's dress and was now wearing trousers, for Bess was looking at him with her head cocked on one side, as if trying to decide whether to press home her new nickname for him. She finally thought better of it.

'Jem's a nice name too,' she said. 'Now I've got to be going, to put on the stew.' She held up the flour sack. 'Da will be pleased with this. Will you be in church, next Sunday, Jem?'

'I 'spect so. You go to church?'

'Of course,' she said, suddenly a little angry, 'you think

57

because we're travellers we can't be Christians? Anyone can be a Christian, if they want to be.'

Jem nodded vigorously, 'Course they can. I didn't mean anything by it.'

Her dog got to its feet as she made a move to go.

'I was at the churchyard, this morning,' she remarked. 'There's a new stone there, since last year. Thomas Timbrell. He wasn't very old when he died.'

'Just comin' up thirteen. He was drowned away, by the river.'

'Oh. Was he your friend?'

'No – well sort of. I wisht he were here now. I wisht it like billy-o. That there Wesley Wickerman – you won't know him but he's a devil, that's for sure – he's drivin' us all into the ground, him and Sir Francis a-tween them.'

'How's that?' she asked, picking a daisy and tickling her lips with it.

'They're tryin' to put the small farmers out of their homes, so Sir Francis can get his hands on the land. We usually beat him to market, see, and he don't like that, so he's hired this bully Wickerman to make us go.' Jem went a little hot as he remembered something else. 'He struck my father too, that Wickerman. Just knocked him down for nothing. Hurt my dad, he did ...'

She looked at him thoughtfully, then said, 'Well, sometimes you get your wishes, and sometimes you don't. It's all dependent on God or the faeries.'

Bess plucked a white-maned dandelion from beside the tow path and blew away the seeds, watching the tiny white parasols drift away on the breeze. A single puff was enough to rid the stem of all its fluff.

'One o'clock,' she said, tossing the stem in the air, while Meg leapt to catch it in her mouth.

Jem snorted, 'What's God got to do with faeries?'

'One's true and the other's not, but nobody knows which.'

'You're supposed to be a Christian, you said.'

Her dark eyes followed his and stared into them.

'I know, but sometimes when I get up of a morning, and the dew is sparkling on the grass round the caravan, I go to fetch the water. The night before, I said my prayers and believed in God, but then I walk through a spinney and find a ring of toadstools where there wasn't none the day before, and if faeries didn't do it, who did?'

'Just growed overnight,' said Jem.

'So quick, and in a perfect round? Anyway, just to be sure, I stand in the faerie ring with the dew cold on my bare toes, and wish for what I prayed for the last night, and sometimes it comes true and sometimes it doesn't. I never know whether God's done it, or the faeries. I always ask both.'

'I don't believe in faeries,' said Jem, 'so that's that.'

'Nor ghosts neither?'

Like most youths, Jem liked to think he needed no beliefs to strengthen his spirit against the vagaries and rigours of the world and the devil.

'None of it, not even God,' he boasted, but even as he spoke the words his heart pounded, and he wondered whether he was going to be struck down where he stood, for blaspheming. He knew that once he got to church that Sunday, he would be praying fervently for forgiveness.

Bess turned to go, but said over her shoulder, 'Oh, I believe in *everything*. It's much better that way. Then you get to look forward to things, instead of always being disappointed.'

He watched her run along the dyke path, her bare feet kicking up daisies. Meg was darting backwards and forwards through her legs, somehow managing to avoid tripping her up. He watched her until all he could see was the bright scarlet in the patterned skirt, way in the distance, stark against some dark green trees. Then she was gone.

'Funny lass, that,' he said to himself. 'Believes in *everything*. Must be crowded in that head of hern, with all those goblins and spooks, and God and all.'

He shook his own head, as if to get rid of any foreign belief that might be in there, out through his ears. Then he began whistling softly and walked in the direction of Pacey's Paddock, where he was to meet his father.

Chapter Ten

Although Wesley Wickerman was generally satisfied with the state of affairs regarding the drowners and their failures, he did not let up in his vigilance for an instant. His master was paying him to crush these people, and that was exactly what he intended to do.

He spent the summer harassing them in any way he could, short of openly sabotaging their system.

'It's really not necessary, is it?' Sir Francis told him. 'What good is a system without the knowledge to run it? It's like having a matched pair of bays and a new high-perch phaeton, but no skilled driver. The horses may be prime bloods, and the coach all the crack, but unless you have a man who can handle the ribbons, they're useless to you. No, Wickerman, you just keep snapping at their heels, man, and we'll see 'em go under before the next year is out.'

Wickerman had a comprehensive spy network throughout the county, consisting of boot boys in the inns, stable grooms, one or two disgruntled farm hands, street urchins and washerwomen. If the drowners held a meeting, he was one of the first to hear about it, and made arrangements to break it up before it had hardly begun.

He frequently walked abroad, showing his broken nose in every part of the landscape, giving the impression that he was everywhere, the eyes and ears of Sir Francis. Wickerman stepped aside for no man on these travels, and went out of his way to intimidate any drowner or farmer he met, especially at the inns.

It had become so that all he had to do was walk into the parlour of The Royal Oak and two or three individuals would hastily drain their tankards and leave, rather than face the humiliation of being taunted by the alley fighter. They knew that none of them were any match for this rawboned, hardheaded man from the streets of East London. His fists and iron-tipped boots, not to mention the hickory stick he carried, were feared above all other physical terrors. Some of the older men had fought in the Napoleonic Wars in their youth, but they confessed they would rather face the French Army than Wesley Wickerman.

'The Frenchies was devious,' remarked Whoffer Riley to his fellow drowners, 'but this 'ere Wickerman is downroight diabolical. He's been sent by the very Devil hisself, you mark my words.'

When the remark got back to Wickerman, by way of a stable lad, he smiled to himself. It was just the sort of talk he liked to encourage. The kind of conversation that will build a myth of invincibility around a man, so that he never need fight at all. All he needed to do was show himself to put the fear of God into all his opponents.

There was one person who was not afraid of him though, and Wickerman decided to do something about that man.

As dusk fell one late summer evening, Wickerman lit a lamp and hung it just inside the cottage window, so that he would be able to follow its light when he returned from The Royal Oak Inn later that night. Sam Teppit, the lock-keeper Wickerman had brought down from Oxford, was instructed not to turn down the lantern if he retired before Wickerman's return to the cottage.

The brittle young man with the long nose and windsail ears nodded gormlessly. Although a good worker, his interest in the world ended on either side of the lock. Wickerman thought he would be asleep on his straw mattress in the woodshed, before the gates of night had finally shut, and the last dim ray of natural light was shut out. Although there were spare bedrooms in the cottage, Wickerman would not let the young man stay inside the house at night.

The tough street fighter would not even doze within easy reach of another man, for fear of assassination while he slumbered. Wickerman was a heavy sleeper and he made sure all the window shutters and doors were securely bolted, the chimney blocked to prevent any small boy being sent inside that way, and the cellar trapdoor barred and locked, before going to his rest. He also kept a blunderbuss loaded with nails and grapeshot, close at hand, ever since his confrontation with James Halliwell.

Wickerman agonised daily on whether to set metal bars at the window in his bedroom, the door of which he always blocked with a huge trunk of oak and iron, or whether to leave it simply shuttered. On the one hand a man intent on murdering him while he was helplessly slumbering, could jemmy the wooden shutters open and enter his bedroom. On the other hand, if someone got into another part of the house, or there was a fire, Wickerman would need an escape route. With bars at the window, he would be trapped in the room.

So each day he went through the torment of changing his mind a dozen times, getting more and more angry with himself as this obsession took greater hold on his fears.

All these preparations, which some might have deemed excessive in the extreme, did not allow Wickerman a peaceful night's rest, for his mind remained alive with disturbing thoughts during the remainder of the dark hours. The main reason for this was that he was forced to sleep in the home of a recently-dead man. He considered that unlucky and unwholesome. It was like wearing a hanged man's jacket. You could smell the ugly scent of death on the garment or in the cottage. While you wore the jacket, or slept in the house, the spirit of the former owner was present.

He left the house, another lamp in hand, and took the path to The Royal Oak. He preferred The Green Man, although that particular inn was farthest away, but going there would have meant passing the graveyard beneath which John Timbrell lay. So he had arranged his meeting in the less comfortable of the two inns.

It was dark when he reached The Royal Oak. He went immediately inside and sat at a table facing the doorway, near to the fireplace which in the summer held only an iron spit. The large rusty skewer was still thick with the grease of ducks and suckling pigs roasted there during last winter.

'A tankard of ale,' he said to the landlady, who stood before him wiping her hands on an apron which appeared to be covered with the same blackened fat which decorated the spit, 'and some pork pieces with bread.'

The repast duly arrived and he began eating and drinking.

When his pot was two-thirds empty of drink a man entered the inn and looked around the room. He was a tall thin character with heavy eyebrows and, when he removed his hat, a red line remained on his forehead where the brim had been pressing. His dark hair hung down to the shoulders of his black coat and remained matted even after he shook his head vigorously, the braids whipping back and forth over his collar.

Wickerman raised a finger and the character nodded and crossed to where he was sitting.

'I'll have the same as this man,' the newcomer told the landlady, 'and be sharp, for I'm both hungry and thirsty, and it puts an edge on my temper.'

The landlady muttered something under her breath but went to prepare the food and drink quickly enough.

'So,' said the newcomer, 'what does Mr Wickerman want with Angel Silke in this armpit of England? I take it you've brought me down here for a job.'

'Not so loud,' growled Wickerman.

Silke looked around.

'There's only two coves in here, asides the old biddy, and they look harmless enough, Wes.'

'They got ears, ain't they? This is a sticky business I'm asking you to do, Angel, and I don't want no witnesses. Now listen close,' his voice fell to a whisper, 'the pigeon's name is Halliwell – James Halliwell. I want you to do him a mischief. There's a tidy purse in it for you.'

Silke scratched his scrawny neck, where the greasy ends of his hair had left a rash.

'A mischief,' he repeated. 'What kind?'

Wesley Wickerman looked the other man directly in the eyes and even before he spoke Angel Silke knew what he had to do.

'I want him turned off.'

Silke smacked his lips, leaning back. His father and the author of his name, was still alive to appreciate the irony of having called a son Angel, who now worked almost exclusively for the legions of hell.

His ale was brought to him along with a plate of pork and bread. He began eating with relish, wiping his fingers on his hair every so often. He ate surprisingly delicately for the kind of man he was, a murderer and a thief, picking up the pork crackling with the longer fingers of his left hand and fastidiously pulling out the stiff pig bristles with the dirty nails of his right, before dropping the food into his mouth as one would a stone down a well.

Wickerman, watching this performance with a disdainful and revolted expression, remarked, 'You're a mighty fiddlesome eater, I'll say that. Fussy as a gallows-bird peckin' at a hanging corpse ...'

Silke paused with a small sprig of pork cracklings halfway to his greasy chin, and went suddenly very pale.

'I'll thank'ee, Wesley Wickerman, to keep such comparisons to yourself. A poor unfortunate dangling from one of them terrible engines of death ain't no humourful matter.'

Wickerman laughed.

'Only those who believe they are going to end up on a scaffold would be worried by such.'

Angel Silke made no reply to this. Finally he had finished his meal and he now leaned over the table, mug in hand, to get closer Wickerman's ear.

'I'll turn 'im off for you, Wes, so long as the bees-and-honey is to my liking. What's his game? One of the local drubbers, eh? Done you a dirty?'

Wickerman shook his head.

'No, he's gentry.'

Silke sat back with a start.

'Gentry? You want me to do a *gentleman*? That's a bit stiff, Wes. I ain't never put a gentleman under the turf before.'

'Come off it, Angel. This is me, Wesley Wickerman. I know exactly who you've done, and there's a good few toffs amongst 'em. Trying to put up the purse? I told you, you'll be seen right.'

Angel's face suddenly split like a turnip under a ploughshare, an expression which only Wickerman amongst the inn's patrons would recognise as a smile.

'That's all right, Wes. You know it is. Anything you got to tell me about him?'

'He's a crackshot with a pistol.'

'I'm glad you told me that. It don't make no mind, because he ain't going to see me, but still that's a consideration.'

'How will you do it?' asked Wickerman. 'I want an accident, mind. We've had a set to, me and him, and I don't want no fingers a-pointin' afterwards.'

'Hmmm.' Silke went into a deep reverie. Finally he said, 'With accidents you got to wait for the right opportunity. And accidents ain't to be trusted, not like a bullet or a knife, or even a garrotte. So, I can't tell you, not 'til it's done, then you'll know soon enough.'

Wickerman suddenly reached forward and gripped the other man's throat with his right hand. His fingers and thumb almost met each other at the back of Angel Silke's neck. The man dropped his ale mug on the table and his eyes bulged.

'Listen, you weasel,' said Wickerman in a low voice, 'don't make any mistakes. If you foul this I'll come looking for you and I'll turn *you* off. You know I'll do it, too.'

He let go the man's throat and his voice became almost pleasant.

'On the other hand, you do good, and I'll see you well compensated.'

Silke coughed and stroked his throat, where small bruises had begun to appear.

'I'll work it right, you see, Wes,' he said.

As Silke was leaving the inn, Wickerman finished a fourth pint of ale and was about to leave himself when a young gypsy girl entered and came up to his table.

'What do you want, girl?' he growled.

Bess said, 'I come for my money. I did what you said, the hole in the dyke. Me and my lurcher Meg, we dug it.'

Wickerman recalled his recent conversation with Sir Francis.

'We're not doing that sort of thing any more,' he said. 'I put the word about. Didn't you hear?'

Bess shook her head.

'Well, here's a coin for you, but don't do any more of that stuff. Just keep your eyes and ears open, and pass any information of note back to me. Understand?'

She took the coin and said, 'That's all right, then, 'cos the boy filled the hole back in, before any water got through.'

'What boy?'

'Said his name was Jem.'

Wickerman grunted. 'One of those dirt-brained drowners. Gave me such a look-through once. No doubt because I gave his old man a facer.' He looked up into her face. 'Well, you just do as you've been told.'

Bess shook her head.

'Don't want to do that no more. This Jem, he seemed a nice boy. When we got here last week, I thought it was you against some people who did you wrong, but *you're* the one who's doing a wrong thing.'

Wickerman went red.

'You watch your tongue, girl. Give me back the coin.'

'No. I earned it.'

The fist that gripped the tankard went white at the knuckles.

'Do as you're told, or you'll be sorry, lass,' he said softly.

She looked at him completely without fear.

'You can bully the farmers, Mr Wickerman, but you touch me and you'll find every gypsy's hand turned against you. Gypsies look after their own kind. All I've got to do is leave a secret mark somewhere near your cottage and you won't know another night of peace.'

He stared into her black eyes and realised it was true.

'Get out of here, get out of my sight.'

She went, but turned at the door and uttered something in a strange gutteral tongue. The tone of her voice was deep and harsh, for a young girl, and the language she used sounded ancient: they were dark mouthings spawned in some forgotten land where beliefs came from souls that lived in shadow.

Then she smiled and was gone, out into the night.

Wickerman gripped his tankard again, but this time his emotion was not anger, it was something quite different.

He knew he'd been cursed.

Chapter Eleven

James Halliwell woke with the sun in his eyes. He had left a gap in the drapes the previous evening, through which a bright shaft of light was piercing the bedroom. It was done for a purpose, since he found the sun a most effective alarm clock, and it was necessary that he be up and about this morning. The faggers were coming from Twyford village to cut the corn in the lower fields. There was a man in charge of them, of course, but James preferred to be at the first day of the fagging himself. He wanted to greet the men and women personally, to show that he appreciated them turning out for the wheat cutting.

He dressed in his riding clothes and then went down to breakfast. His brother and sister-in-law were still in bed, but his father was at the table.

'Good morning, Father,' he said. 'A fine July day. Will you be taking a walk?'

Squire Peter Matthew Halliwell, turned seventy a week previously, grunted something to the ham on his plate, as if he were talking to his breakfast rather than his son.

'But', replied James, 'even a walk around the box garden would be better than nothing.'

Mr Halliwell informed his grilled tomatoes that he was bored with the box garden. The tomatoes remained silently sympathetic to this remark. They were gracefully impassive.

'In that case at least ask one of the servants to provide you with a seat on a shaded part of the lawn, so that you might take some fresh air,' James said.

Mr Halliwell grumbled to a one-eyed haddock that his son was bullying him again. Why, he told the smoked fish, could not people leave him alone in his own household? Why did they fuss and flummox over him, when he was perfectly happy just sitting in his chair in the library and thinking.

'Because we're concerned for your welfare,' remarked James. 'It's what you think *about* that worries us. You sit and brood, and you're not at all happy, despite what you say. Now we don't expect you to dance around the house singing Irish folk songs, but it just isn't healthy for you to hide yourself in a dark dusty room, thinking of Mother. We all miss her, you more than most, of course, but we must accept her death as inevitable and try to get on with living once again.'

The old man lifted his eyes to meet with those of his son's and James read the misery in them.

James said softly, 'I know, I know, Father, but we love you too, and we don't want to see you pine into sickness. Mother wouldn't have wanted that to happen, and you know it too. She would scold you, if she were able, for the way in which you have been treating yourself. Please *try* to get out of the house today, if only for half an hour?'

The haddock received the faintest of nods.

James went from the breakfast room to the stables where he assisted the groom in saddling his grey, Sheba. Once the horse was ready, he set off down the short driveway to the woodland track which he took most mornings when exercising Sheba. As usual he intended to gallop her across the open fields beyond the far spinney, then strike out for the lower corn fields.

The mare was so familiar with the route James did not need to tell her what to do, nor where to do it. She knew exactly at what point to walk, to trot, to break into a canter, and when to extend herself into a full-blooded gallop.

Oaks, elms, hawthorns, hornbeams and sycamores drifted by as Sheba trotted along the leafy path through the woods. James passed a stream where a group of teasel-gatherers were collecting the hooked bracts of the plant, which were used to raise the nap on woollen garments. He bid them good morning as they raised their heads amongst the two-metre high teasels, nodding to him below the height of the flower.

When they were past the stream, Sheba broke into a canter,

knowing that around the next batch of hawthorns was the four-barred gate she would have to jump, almost sight unseen. She did it most mornings and had never balked at the task. Since the field behind the gate was off the main track there was little likelihood of meeting someone and James felt perfectly safe in taking a blind corner without shouting a warning. In fifteen years there had never been a single soul to cause him concern at this point in his familiar ride. In any case his almost daily route was well known to the local people and only a stranger would fail to recognise any danger at that particular place at this certain time.

'Good girl,' said James as Sheba took the curve in the path, perfectly positioned for rounding the thickly-clustered hawthorns and then jumping the gate.

As they swished by the squat thorny trees both creatures prepared themselves for the leap over the roughly-hewn bars of the gate.

Suddenly, the obstacle was before them, but instead of launching herself, Sheba started and twisted sharply sideways. There on the gate, not three metres away, sat a young boy. In the second before he was thrown, James was looking into the cool calm eyes of the youth, who sat with his feet tucked under the top bar of the gate, his hands gripping the horizontal pole, one either side of him. He seemed about to fling himself into the path of the horse.

Sheba lost her balance and her forelegs went from under her. James and his saddle were abruptly divorced from one another and he flew through the air to land on his shoulder by the hedge. With all the wind knocked out of him, he lay there for a few moments in a dazed state.

Once he had recovered, he climbed to his feet, looking for the youngster he had almost injured. Only Sheba's instinct had saved the boy from serious harm. The youth was gone, however, and Sheba was already upright, standing quietly with the reins dangling from her bridle.

'Now where did he go?' James muttered, staring around at

the empty landscape beyond the gate. Leaving Sheba to graze, he walked around the hawthorn clump to look along the woodland path, but there was no one in sight. 'Up a tree perhaps?' He glanced in that direction, but he did not really believe the boy could have climbed so quickly. In any case, the nearest trees were the hawthorns, covered in spines. The youth would have to be a clever climber to shin up one of those without causing himself distress.

James decided the boy must have been afraid that James would take his riding crop to him, for causing the horse to balk, and had run and hidden somewhere.

'You can come out if you wish,' cried James, 'I don't intend to punish you. It was as much my fault as yours, and there's been no harm done.'

There was no answer and James shrugged. He retrieved Sheba's reins and mounted again. Once he was in the saddle, however, he could see over the top of the gate, directly into the field beyond. His blood was chilled by what he saw.

Right on the spot where Sheba would have landed, had they taken the jump as usual, was a huge oak-tree bough. The end that had been joined to the bole of the tree was pointing away from the gate, while the branch ends were facing towards it. The broken tips of the branches, some of them as thick as James's wrist, were jagged points. They presented a ragged phalanx of spearmen, ready to pierce the flesh of anyone who took the gate blindly on horseback.

Sheba would have been severely injured, perhaps killed. James himself would have suffered a similar fate.

'We've been lucky, old girl,' he whispered, patting Sheba's neck. 'If that boy hadn't been there …'

Suddenly he saw something in the field which made him flare with anger. He dismounted and tied Sheba's reins to the gates, before climbing over it. Once in the field he walked through the branches to look at the stem of the bough.

He had of course believed that the bough was there by accident, torn by a strong wind from one of the oak trees that

72

provided shade for grazing cattle on hot summer days. Now he could see that was not so. The presence of the bough was no accident. There was a long snaking groove in the turf leading to a tree some thirty metres away. *The bough had been dragged in front of the gate.*

James stood and pondered, hoping that in fact someone had attempted to drag the bough back to the village, to use it as firewood, and had underestimated its weight. Perhaps the boy he had seen? James wanted to believe that there had not been a deliberate attempt to harm someone.

However, when he tried to lift the obstacle, he found it difficult. It was all he could do to drag it out of the way and run it up against the hedge where it would not interfere with riders such as himself. No boy the size of the one he had seen sitting on the gate could have moved that bough more than a half a metre or a metre at most.

Some irresponsible man, or men, had been playing a dangerous game. James resolved to make enquiries in the village and find out whether the local inn had turned out some drunks late last night, or whether there was a gang of strangers in the area, perhaps hoping to join the faggers. If his head man had turned such men away, it might well be that they had attempted to get their own back for being refused work.

By the time he reached the faggers in the lower fields James was boiling with fury. He snapped out a few questions to his head man.

'Has anyone come in the direction of the house this morning? Who took the path through the wood? I saw a boy there, does anyone know him?'

His head man stared at him, mouth agape, unused to seeing the young master in such a foul mood.

'None that I heard of, Master James,' he eventually replied. He turned to the villagers. 'Who took the woodland path this morn?'

'Oi did,' snapped one of the women, 'but oi put it back again, after I'd used it.'

73

There was laughter and despite his anger James couldn't help but smile at the humour.

'No one has seen any strangers in the area this morning?' he enquired, once they were silent again.

There was a solemn shaking of heads. The faggers hooked their sickles over their shoulders and folded their arms, looking to one another for support.

James explained. 'Someone deliberately left an oak bough in a place where it was likely to do great harm to any rider using the woodlands path. If you know anything about it, speak up please.'

A thin young man James recognised as being the son of the innkeeper stepped forward.

'Begging your pardon, Master James, I see a man last night in our inn. He was London folks, by his speech.'

'Is he staying at the inn?'

The young man shook his head.

'Left this very morning, early. Up with the rooster, he was, and away.'

'Can you describe this man?'

'He were tall and lean like, but strong looking. Face like a blunt hatchet. Dark eyes, dark hair. Talked familiar with Father like he was friends from childhood, though Father said he'd not seen the man afore last night. Come to think on it, he were askin' after people around Twyford, and your name was mentioned in passing. Said he was just curious and thought he knowed one or two folks hereabouts. That's as much as I can tell.'

'Thank you,' said James quietly. 'It may be that this man had nothing whatsoever to do with the oak bough, but I should like to talk to him in any case. Did he by any chance ask after my movements?'

'May have. Can't remember. Didn't hear all he spoke of.'

James said, 'Let me know if you hear of him again.'

'I will,' replied the young man.

The return ride to the house passed without incident, though

James was naturally quite wary. He found his own father sitting out in a chair on the lawn, looking embarrassed and out of sorts.

'Well done, Father,' he called, when he strolled back from the stables. 'That's the way.'

'Feel damned foolish,' muttered the old man to a geranium in the nearest flower bed. 'Anyone sees me sitting out here will think me mad.'

'No they won't', replied James. 'All our friends know that I've been trying to get you out into the fresh air.'

His father made a face, then asked James's feet whether they had had an enjoyable ride.

'Yes, thank you. No problems down there that I can see. Our man has everything in hand. I'm delighted you're taking an interest.'

'Good, good,' mumbled the old man to his left shoulder, and picked up a book of verse that lay on the grass.

James crept away, hoping his father would spend at least another hour in the open. James had a visit to plan, to the Almshouse of Noble Poverty at St Cross, where he had promised to help in the restoration of the cruciform chapel.

Chapter Twelve

The Hospital of St Cross, not an establishment for the sick and dying but a place which offers *hospitality* to travellers, is situated a mile or so south of Winchester near to the water meadows. There live 'the Brothers' – twenty-five impoverished old men, twelve of them dressed in red, the rest in black – whose lives are closing and to whom St Cross offers charity.

At St Cross the wayfarer can receive nourishment to assist him on his journey: bread, cheese and ale. All he has to do is enter the Beaufort Gatehouse and ask for the wayfarers' dole. St Cross is a place of tall chimneys like soldiers on parade; a large courtyard; a church; a communal kitchen; beautiful gardens and an ambulatory – a place of peace.

James Halliwell saddled Sheba and rode towards St Cross the morning after his narrow escape from injury, or perhaps even death. He was wary, keeping his eyes open for anything unusual. It had occurred to him after his talk with the innkeeper's son that perhaps the oak bough had been left on the far side of the gate, not as an act of negligence, but had been placed there specifically to harm James Halliwell. He was not sure about this, but there was no reason to dismiss the idea out of hand.

He rode to St Cross by way of St Catherine's Hill, because he liked the view of the river from that point. On its crest he met a youth, chin in hands, deep in thought. The boy looked up, startled, when the shadow of the horse passed over him. He had obviously been day-dreaming so much he had not heard the soft sound of Sheba's hooves on the springy turf.

'Good morning,' said James.

The boy jumped up and said nervously, 'Mornin', Mr Halliwell.'

James reined his mount, and frowned.

'Do I know you?' he asked.

'Jem, sir. Jem Blunden. You spoke to me after visitin' Martha Timbrell's cottage one time. It was about Tom – Tom Timbrell.'

The memory of the meeting by the lock-keeper's cottage filtered into James's mind. Yes of course, the youngster who claimed to have been an enemy of Tom Timbrell. Was he still feeling guilty over what appeared to be just a falling out of two school friends? Sitting here brooding on the past?

'What are you thinking of?' he asked Jem. 'Not still Tom?'

Jem hung his head.

'No, sir, I done wisht him back three times now – yesterday mornin' were the last time – and no Tom has come. I can't do no more than that, can I, sir?'

Something flashed through James's mind. He leaned forward in his saddle to study the youth's face.

'Listen, Jem,' he said slowly, 'you weren't by any chance near Twyford yesterday, were you?'

Jem took a step back and shook his head.

'No, sir,' he said emphatically. 'Not me.'

James was suspicious.

'Why are you looking so worried, Jem? What are you afraid of?'

'You asked me like something was wrong, like someone stole something. I weren't nowhere near Twyford, sir, an' that's a fact. I were with Bess ...'

'Bess?'

'A gypsy girl, Mr Halliwell.' Then he added quickly, 'an' she didn't steal nothing neither. Just because she's one of them, it don't mean she's a thief. We was just out walking along the towpath, that's all.'

James wondered whether the boy was telling the truth, because he looked guilty about something. Then it occurred to him that Jem's family might not approve of him having a gypsy girl for a friend and perhaps this was the reason for Jem's embarrassment.

77

'You weren't sitting on a gate at the end of a woodland path then, early yesterday morning?' he said.

Jem shook his head again.

'No, sir. Not me. Nor Bess neither.'

'No,' James smiled, 'I know it wasn't Bess. It was definitely a youth around about your age. Perhaps a little younger. For heaven's sakes, stop looking so anxious, Jem. I'm not going to accuse you of anything. I'm simply trying to trace a youngster who might be able to help me find out who tried ... well, never mind now. I'll bid you good day, Jem.'

'Good day, Mr Halliwell.'

James squeezed Sheba's flanks gently with his knees and the mare trotted on, down the gradual slope towards the river and St Cross. He rode over the Itchen by way of the stone arched bridge. Below the cool green world of pike and trout sparkled in the sunlight. James thought briefly of how pleasant it would be to go fishing, instead of working on the ceiling of the chapel, but he had promised North, the Master of St Cross, that he would help with the restoration work. James had a strong sense of duty.

Leaving Sheba to graze on the water meadow outside St Cross, James entered through the arched gate and made his way directly to the chapel. He had no desire to run into Master North, who was not a pleasant man and one of the first to use his position as Master to exploit the hospital. North had been appointed by his father, then the Bishop of Winchester, who also wrung as much profit out of his cathedral and diocese as possible, and had rarely visited Winchester during his forty years as its spiritual head.

The church of St Cross, however, needed work on it and since Master North was not prepared to pay for the labour it had to be done by the Brethren, all of whom were too old to climb ladders or scaffolding. Master North had approached the young gentry in and around St Cross and asked for their help. He was shameless about doing so and though he was despised for his avarice, most people realised that the church would fall to bits and all Master North would do about it would be to sell the loose blocks of stone at a profit to himself.

Thus James had agreed to do his bit.

On entering the cruciform chapel, James stared around him. Another local man, one of the drowners, had been in earlier to erect a makeshift rickety-looking scaffolding for James to climb up to the ceiling where the last of the whitewash needed to be removed. In the seventeenth century another Master of St Cross, one Dr Markland, had had a passion for whitewash. He had covered the whole church with it, hiding all the natural beauty of the stonework and woodwork. It had subsequently taken centuries to remove the offending layers of wash. The ceilings had clung to vestiges of white longer than the chapel walls and Norman pillars, they being difficult to reach to remove the substance.

James put on a white smock to protect his clothing and then began to climb the unsteady scaffolding. Around him, splashing on the pews, the altar cloth and the stone floors, were the colours from medieval stained-glass windows. One of them, the bird-beak window, was unique in all England. The whole place was musty and damped with silence, the shafts of sunlight turning dust motes to precious-looking specks, settling on the lectern which was carved with a parrot's head to remind readers to recite from the heart, not repeat the words like a hollow mimic.

One of the Brothers came into the chapel as James reached the top of the scaffolding and began scraping away at the ingrained whitewash. James looked down. It was one of the de Blois, in black, Brother Nathan.

'Good morning, Brother Nathan,' called James.

Brother Nathan was by this time in the Lady Chapel and out of sight. He came back out and looked nervously around the church, obviously seeing nothing.

'I'm up here, Nathan,' said James, expecting the other man to look heavenwards.

Instead, Nathan looked around him wildly, failed to take

notice of the scaffolding or did not consider its significance, and finally fell to his knees. He then clasped his hands in front of him, and cried in falteringly rapturous tones:

'Speak, Lord, thy servant heareth!'

James could not help but smile to himself.

'It's not the Lord who speaks, but James Halliwell,' he said. 'Nathan, please raise your eyes slowly to heaven and you'll find they will rest eventually on me.'

Brother Nathan did as he was bid, the anxiety obvious in his wizened features. He looked as though he believed he was ready to die at the hand of the Almighty. No doubt he thought his hour was nigh and that the messenger angel had come in the form of his friend James Halliwell. When those failing, misty, brown eyes finally rested on James's features, the old man whispered, 'Are you come to take me away, white angel of light?'

James suddenly remembered two things: one, he was dressed in a white flowing smock, much like an angel down from the clouds would be expected to dress, and two, Brother Nathan was extremely short-sighted. Covered with the colours from the windows and the suffused sunlight swirling the dust around his form he must indeed have appeared to be a celestial creature.

'Nathan,' he said gently, 'I'm not an angel, or a spirit — it really is me, James Halliwell. I'm up here restoring the ceiling. Please get off your knees. All I wanted to do was bid you good morning.'

Nathan squinted and glared ferociously, then climbed to his feet, his old bones creaking in the silence of the church.

'What's to do? Trying to frighten me, eh? Well, it didn't work, you young loon. I was jesting along with you, see?'

'Of course you were,' replied James, realising the old man was trying to rescue his dignity. 'I see that now.'

Nathan then shuffled back towards the Lady Chapel, grumbling and glowering at all around him. James smiled to himself. It had not been his intention to upset the old man, but all the same, he had been a humorous sight, down there on his knees, expecting to be wafted to God's bosom at any moment.

James worked steadily for the next two hours, scraping away at the whitewash which had hardened to rock and had become part of the stonework itself over the centuries. His hair was covered in white flecks, like dandruff, and the chippings got into his eyes and mouth, causing him some distress.

At one point his scraper raised a shower of sparks and dust went directly into his eyes, making him drop his tool. It fell, clattering through the wooden scaffolding, and struck the floor below. James took a kerchief out of his pocket and tried to clear his eyes, which were watering profusely. There was a sound below, of someone scuttling down the aisle, and he called, 'Nathan, is that you? Can you help me? I can't see properly. Could you guide me down with your voice.'

There was a cackle of crow-like laughter.

A harsh voice cried, 'No, it ain't Nathan, whoever he is. It's the Devil, and I've come to take your soul.'

James, still unable to see, said, 'That must be Nathan. Are you trying to pay me back, for that trick you thought I played on you this morning?'

Suddenly the scaffolding wobbled dangerously, as if it were being shaken.

'Hey!' cried James, alarmed, and he clutched blindly at the rail for support.

'I told you who it was. You ain't listenin', are you? I'm Satan hisself and I've come for you, Halliwell. The gate didn't get you, but the scaffold will.' There was another crow-like laugh.

A sudden wrench followed this sound and to James's consternation and terror, he found himself flying through the air as the scaffolding collapsed beneath him. He opened his eyes wide, as he fell, their soreness suddenly unimportant, pushed aside by the greater danger of almost certain death on the stone floor below. In that second he saw his attacker, a lean hatchet-faced man, strong-looking, with dark eyes and hair. Then James crashed and his world went black.

* * *

When he opened his eyes the first thing he saw was not St Peter, but Brother Nathan's concerned expression.

'Am I alive?' he croaked to the grey-haired old man.

'Alive, but hardly well,' replied Nathan. 'You took a bad fall there, my boy.'

James was aware of lumpy objects underneath his back, their corners digging into his flesh.

'What ... where did I fall?'

Nathan said, 'You were lucky. You landed on a pile of prayer books stacked between the pews. Brother Harold, one of the Beauforts, had promised to put them away. What a blessing for you that he's a no-good lazy old fool and is probably still sleeping in his bed.'

'I'm glad of that,' said James, but groaned when he tried to stand up. 'I'm bruised all over and my head feels as if it's twice its size.'

'Anything broken?' asked Nathan, doing his frail best to help James to his feet.

'Not that I can feel. Where did he go?'

'I saw no one. Who do you mean?'

'The man with the laugh, the man that tried to kill me, yesterday and today. I must find him before he tries a third time. I can't put myself in God's hands every time – I shall be sure to slip through his fingers at some point.'

He steadied himself, having regained his feet. He ached all over and his head was pounding. Touching his brow gingerly he found an egg there, just below the skin.

'Nasty bump,' remarked Nathan, 'but better than a broken neck.'

'Indeed,' agreed James. 'Can I rest somewhere until my orientation returns. I'm feeling somewhat giddy at the moment and it's a foolish experience. Do you mind?' He leaned on Nathan, who helped him out of the church and into one of the Brother's quarters, where the old man gave him some brandy and administered a cold compress to his head. A second

Brother, a physician of sorts, was fetched from the infirmary on the upper storey, and he made sure there were no broken bones.

When James felt well enough, he made his way homeward at a slow pace, on Sheba. She seemed to understand that her master was not feeling too good and, though she was used to being trotted or cantered part of the way home, remained easy in her stride for the whole journey.

For his part, James was thinking. He was going through a list of his enemies, to try to discover who would want him dead. The list was fairly short, but two names stood out beyond the rest. Sir Francis Alderton and his man Wesley Wickerman. He could prove nothing, of course, unless he caught the perpetrator of the deed.

No doubt the fellow would be on his way out of the country by now, and would lose himself in the backstreets of some city. The thing to do would be to let Wickerman know that he was known to be behind the plot. That might prevent future attempts on his life.

When he arrived home, James took a bath. Then he sat at his writing table and composed a short note. It read:

'*Wickerman.*

I think you should be aware that a hired murderer revealed the names of his masters to me.

James Halliwell.'

James then sent for his stable boy and had him deliver the note to the lock-keeper's cottage.

Chapter Thirteen

Wesley Wickerman woke to the sound of loud bangings on his cottage door. The knock sounded hostile: the knock of soldiers come to take a man to prison or execution; the knock of hostile neighbours come to drag a man away to tar and feather him; the knock of the Devil come for his dues.

Wickerman pulled the blanket up to his chin, as if this might protect him. He lay there for a few minutes staring up into the darkness, wondering if the world had ended and this was actually a messenger calling for his attendance at the Judgement. Then thin lines of light shone around the edges of his bedroom door, and he realised that Sam Teppit, not yet gone to his bed in the woodshed, was answering the knock.

He heard the locks being drawn on the outer door, the wooden latch being lifted. He heard the door being swung open. These noises were followed by mutterings which filled Wickerman with misgivings. Who could be calling at the cottage at this time of night? Who would dare, apart from his master?

The outer door was closed, the clatter of horse's hooves sounded on the stony path outside. The light around the edge of the door became brighter and brighter, until a tapping, scratching noise was heard on its thick panels.

'Sir? Sir?'

It was Sam Teppit.

'What is it?' said Wickerman.

'A note it is, sir, delivered by the hand of a man up from Twyford.'

'Push it under the door.'

There was a slithering sound as Teppit did as he was ordered. Then the light faded, went out, and all was peaceful once more. Wesley Wickerman left the piece of paper where it was and attempted to go to sleep again.

Wickerman woke the next morning and dressed hurriedly. He had had an uncomfortable night and was in bad sorts. Opening the shutters, he glanced towards the door and saw the note. He picked it up and read it by the grey light of dawn that filtered through the dirty windows.

His face reddened as his eyes scanned the words. Then he screwed the paper up in his fist and tossed it into the corner.

'That blamed fool!' he muttered. 'Should have known better than to hire a nincompoop like Angel Silke.'

He left the cottage an hour later, stick in hand, and made his way to The Green Man, where Silke was staying. When he arrived at the inn, Silke was still in his bed, so Wickerman asked if someone would 'rouse the sluggard'. Then he ordered himself some breakfast.

Silke joined him in a half an hour.

'What's to do?' asked Silke.

'You were seen,' growled Wickerman. 'Don't deny it!'

Silke looked puzzled.

'Who saw me? Nobody saw me, not except ...' Then he stopped and looked into Wickerman's eyes, before saying quietly, 'Ain't he gone then? I thought I'd turned him off for sure.'

'He must be alive, mustn't he, if he sends me notes in the middle of the night?'

Silke said, 'Maybe it's a trick? Maybe he's dead and they're trying to catch us together?'

He glanced nervously at the windows of the inn, as if he expected to see accusing faces there.

'They got no proof, have they?' said Wickerman. 'Not unless you talked while you worked? Did you talk, Silke?'

Wickerman tapped the tabletop with the bulbous handle of his hickory stick.

Angel Silke drew back in his seat.

'Not me, Wes. I don't carp. You know me.'

'I think I do, but I ain't sure. We got to speak this out, Silke. Not in here though. Too many ears. Pay the landlord and meet me out in the yard.'

Silke gave a faint smile.

'I wasn't thinkin' of settling me whack, Wes. Not with some cabbage-head of a country landlord. I was goin' to skip ...'

'Not this time. I drink in this inn. I don't want to have to answer questions every time I come here for a toddy. You pay your damned bill and meet me in the yard.'

Silke joined him outside and the two of them set off over the chalk downs, travelling north. They followed a rough flint road for part of the way, then Wickerman branched off on to a small track which led to a disused shepherd's hut with drystone walls and no roof.

There was a well outside the hut, which was also no longer in use. A rank smell issued from the depths of this hole, whose brickwork and opening had disappeared beneath moss and fern. It was like one of those jungle traps natives set for wild animals: a pit into which the unknowing might fall.

Wickerman stopped just beside the well, knowing that Silke had not seen the danger. He motioned for the other man to stand beside him, and when he did so, Wickerman clutched at his arm. The pair of them were standing on the very edge of the waterless pit, only one of them aware of its existence.

'Silke.'

'What?' asked the other, then wrinkled his thin nose to show he disliked the stench coming from the immediate vicinity.

Wickerman asked abruptly, 'What happened? With Halliwell, I mean?'

Angel Silke explained his two attempts at killing James Halliwell over the previous few days. He added that Halliwell had seen him, just before falling from the scaffolding, and if the man was alive he could identify his attacker.

'He'll have me in the lockup, so he will, if he claps eyes on me again. I need something now, Wes. To get me back to London. I ain't got nothin' in me pocket, after spillin' out to that landlord. You got to sub me.'

'And what if I don't?'

Angel Silke's eyes hardened.

'Then I might 'ave to speak me mind, in all conscience, if you get my meanin'.'

Wickerman nodded, mildly.

'So, even if I do sub you, and you gets caught, you'll spill out, is that it?'

Angel Silke said nothing. He knew he could never convince Wesley Wickerman that he would not speak to the police if he were caught and identified by James Halliwell. It was best that Wickerman believed the only way to keep him quiet was to give him the money to get back to London and relative safety. Once he was back in Wilde Alley, why, no one would be able to lay a hand on him. The district there was so thick with thieves it was a forest of footpads. The houses around Wilde Alley were riddled with priest holes and secret tunnels.

'Give me the billies, Wes,' he said, his voice now more demanding as he put out his hand for the money. He wrinkled his nose at the odour coming from the grasses at his feet. 'This place stinks o' rotten meat. I'd rather be out of it.'

Wesley Wickerman stood staring at Angel Silke for a moment, then said, 'There's a louse on your collar.'

Silke reached up with his left hand and felt around the collar of his coat.

'Where?' he asked, screwing his head round, first one way, then the other, trying to find the louse with his eyes.

There was no answer. Instead, Wesley Wickerman twisted the knob of his hickory. He swiftly withdrew the blade of a sword from his stick and stepped up close to the other man, while Silke's attention was on other things.

The sound of a rook *carking* as it flew overhead, drowned any human cry which might have pierced the still air of the downs.

* * *

Wickerman looked around, quickly, but there was no one in sight over the downs. He slid the blade back into its hickory scabbard. Then he gave the handle a short sharp twist to lock it into place.

The well had not had water in it for a generation. He rearranged the ferns that had been over the entrance to the black hole, so that any bent or broken fronds were now back in place.

There was a dead sheep in the well, which accounted for the smell. A local shepherd had been complaining about its loss in The Green Man, about three weeks ago, which was how Wickerman came to learn of the well's existence.

By the time anybody came to investigate further, if they ever did, they would be hard put to find any incriminating marks on Silke. Most likely they would think that Silke had stumbled on the hole by accident, fallen in, and struck his head on the stones below.

Chapter Fourteen

The drowners were still no nearer to discovering the secret of the water meadows, and most went into their second winter with despair in their hearts. They dreaded the coming of the spring when they would once again have to guess which sluices to open, which to leave closed, and all the intricacies of timing that went with a good drowning. They foresaw the water meadows, over-flooded or iced, being useless to them once again.

North, the Bishop's son and Master of St Cross, acted as a watching agent for Sir Francis Alderton. The hospital was very close to the water meadows and he saw the gloom that winter had cast upon the tenant farmers. He reported this in a note to Sir Francis.

'They mooch about their fields, looking downcast and weary, sometimes glancing up at St Catherine's chapel, on the hill, as if they hope to find comfort there.'

Such reports obviously pleased Sir Francis immensely and he stood in front of his great marble fireplace and whistled softly to himself, his happiness derived from someone else's misery. Wesley Wickerman's reports were no less cheering and Sir Francis decided that this was the year that would see an end to his lowly rivals, the tenant farmers of the Itchen, once and for all. He was happy. He was happy.

Freezing winds, thin and keen as cheesewire, cut across the county, bringing deer to their knees. Sharp frosts gripped the lungs of field mice and squeezed them empty of breath. It was one of the coldest winters people had known and firewood became scarce. Old men huddled around the stoves in the trading stores, telling stories of winters that froze dogs in half-stride and brought birds down out of the skies as solid lumps, to thud on to the earth. They spoke of eggs that clunked into the pan and had to be thawed before frying, and milk that iced over between cowshed and farmhouse.

Jem Blunden moved through this terrible winter in a blanket-smock, looking like some strange monk from a mountainous land. He walked the downs, tracking his own footprints over the still ridges with their skeletons of trees. The air was so cold it froze minds as well as bodies and Jem's thinking led him nowhere.

Apart from worrying about the drowning in the spring, he was missing Bess, the gypsy girl, of whom he had become very fond. He was thinking that perhaps, one day, he would ask her to marry him, though he wondered what his family would do about such a thing. His father did not approve of gypsies. Still, that was a long way in the future, for he was only just fifteen and nowhere near ready for matrimony and its responsibilities yet.

One morning Jem crossed the water meadows to some trees by the river. There he stood staring at the river water rushing by, cold-looking and forbidding. He took out his penknife and began carving the initial B on the trunk of an old elm. He followed this with the letter J and then proceeded to cut a heart around the two letters, when he was suddenly aware of someone standing nearby.

He jumped back from the tree and his face reddened.

'I weren't ... it's just ... why was you spying on me?' he accused the figure, mortified at being caught at such a sissy pastime.

The other, a boy some two to three years younger than Jem, stepped forward. He had a pale thin face which was deep down inside his overcoat collar. His lips were red, as if he had been eating wild berries, and a dark lock of hair had fallen over his forehead.

He regarded Jem with eyes as dark as Bess's.

'I weren't spying,' he said. 'I just saw you walking through the trees and I come to meet you.'

Jem nodded, furiously.

'Walkin', yes, that's what I were a-doing. Just walkin', and I'll thank you to remember that.'

Jem had suddenly become aware that the boy was no match for him physically, and he could intimidate him with his size. Then something else struck him.

'You come to meet me? Now why would you want to do a thing like that? I don't know you.'

'That's true,' said the boy, eagerly, 'but you'm familiar with my family. We was sent to Norfolk, to a lock there. Me and my brothers and sisters. I heard the drowners was in trouble and I come down here to help.'

Jem's eyes opened wide.

'You one of them Timbrells?'

The boy nodded eagerly.

'That's right. And you be Jem? My brother Benjamin spoke on you. Said you knowed each other.'

There were so many Timbrells it was hard to keep track of them all. It was not surprising that Jem should not know this one, since he was a good two or three years younger than Jem himself. Such gaps in age, at their time of life, were chasms only bridged by accident.

'Ben, yes. But it were Tom what were being apprenticed to the Master Drowner. What do you know about such things?'

'Ah, well, you see,' the boy stepped forward and smiled, 'I used to listen in, when Dad were talking to Tom. I heared a lot of things, though I were always bein' told to buzz off, and not to mind the business of others. I were real taken with the drowning, though, and I've got a quick head for such.

'Now, when word reached us that you needed help, my mum said, "Matt, you get on down there, to Hampshire, and see what you can do for the drowners there, before that Sir Francis has stole all their lands ..." '

'That'll never happen,' growled Jem.

'No, I should hope not,' said the bright-eyed Matt.

Jem regarded this newcomer for some time, before saying

91

rather impolitely, 'You can't stay at my house. We got no room, not with the new baby bein' born last week. There's scarce enough room for the rest of us.'

'I don't care about that,' replied Matt. 'I've found a hut up on the downs – old shepherd's place made of good stone. I laid some branches over the roof and put some turf up there, to keep out the winter. I'll be snug up there.'

Jem said, 'An' what will you eat?'

'I thought of that,' said Matt, after a second, 'and I decided to get took on at The Green Man as a boot boy, just in the early mornin's. Polishin' boots'll keep me warm, and fed too.'

His dark eyes regarded Jem, as the youth thought this over. It seemed this *was* a bright youngster in front of him, and if Martha Timbrell had sent him down from Norfolk, he must know something about the drowning. They had to keep this a secret though, between the two of them, or Wickerman would find out and cause trouble.

'You better not go spreading this around,' he said to Matt, 'otherwise Wesley Wickerman will find some way to drive you back to Norfolk.'

Matt said, 'I were thinking that maybe you could pass on the whys and wherefores, to the drowners, once spring comes around again. I tell you, and you tell them. That would be a method of keepin' it from Wesley Wickerman, though you'll be in danger from him. Had you thought on that?'

Jem puffed out his chest.

'I'll not be afraid of that man, when the time comes. I'll be closin' on sixteen years. That's well into being a man, true or not?'

'True,' replied Matt, 'but there be no lack of full growed men afraid of Wickerman.'

'I'll not be one of 'em.'

The other boy smiled with his cherry-red lips.

'Good. There we have it, then. I'll do the telling, you do the listening, then you can see the drowners get it right.'

A thought came to Jem.

'You *do* know a bit on it? I mean, I don't want to be a fool when the tellin' time comes. I'll have to say it was me what found out about the scheme old John used, and if it all goes wrong, why, I'll be the one to blame, seemingly.'

'What's best? We try it and fail, or we let the men just drown the fields with no thought to plans, and it all goes wrong just the same?'

Jem nodded. This Matt Timbrell spoke a lot of sense and there was no getting around that. The drowners were bound to do it badly, with no advice, so what was there to lose? Only Jem Blunden's pride, and that was no great thing against what his glory would be if the scheme worked. Why, he would be exalted amongst his kin and kind. He would be a hero, even to his mother, who had never considered that he would amount to much. She loved him (she said) but he was just a boy.

'We'll do it,' said Jem. 'Here, take my hand on it.'

The other boy moved off quickly, walking towards the river.

'I can't stop no longer. I promised the landlord of The Green Man I would tell him today about being his boot boy.'

Jem cried, 'When will I see you again?'

'I'll find you,' called Matt, over his shoulder as he ran along the frosty path. 'Next week, we'll go out into the meadows, and talk on some things. You've got a lot to learn 'fore the spring comes.'

That's true enough, thought Jem, digging his hands deep into his pockets. It had taken young Tom Timbrell three years to get a rough working of the plan in his head, so Jem had been told by Alex Blunden, his father. Now Jem was expected to understand the scheme in just a few weeks! Still, this boy Matt seemed much brighter than himself, brighter even than Tom had been, so maybe he would be a good teacher and get things across easily.

'Half the battle is having a good teacher,' muttered Jem to himself. 'The other half is for me to listen in hard.'

He knocked his knuckles against his skull.

'Got to get it in there. Got to listen in hard, for the first time in my life, and not be so wooden. Whoffer Riley's got wooden limbs, while I got a wooden head.'

The difficulty lay not only with learning what Matt had to offer, but also in persuading the drowners that he was knowledgeable enough to oversee the drowning. Matt had said he did not want his identity to be disclosed, which meant that somehow Jem had to get the men to believe that he had some sort of insight into the machinations of the drowning. He had to be careful though. He didn't want to be accused of being a witch or a sorcerer. Country folk were superstitious and he might find himself the centre-piece of an ugly village scene.

Whoffer Riley! Now there was a man who was scared of nothing and nobody. A bit of near magic would not worry him. Despite being half timber, and having to rub linseed oil on parts of his body to make them supple, Whoffer Riley commanded a lot of respect in the county. Once Jem had got an idea of what drowners needed to do, he would enlist the aid of Whoffer, telling the old man that the drowning had 'come to him natural', like swimming to an otter.

Whoffer was one of those men who fell in with the existence of natural human talents. Some men were born to be coopers, their hands made by God to shave and steam planks into staves. Some men were put on the earth to be shipwrights, or farmers, or artists, or writers. Jem would convince Whoffer that he had master-drowner skills locked in his skull, knocking to come out.

'That's what I'll do. I'll get Whoffer Riley to stand on side of me,' Jem said to himself.

He climbed a gate to cross the last field before his home and a realisation suddenly came to him. James Halliwell, so the story had got around the villages, had been saved from death by a strange youth sitting on his gate.

'I bet that was Matt Timbrell,' said Jem. 'I bet anything that was Matt Timbrell saved Mr Halliwell.'

Jem was changing his mind about himself. He used to think

himself not very bright, but all sorts of schemes and realisations were flowing through his head now. It just showed what desperation did to someone. It unblocked all the bunged-up holes in his brain, and let the ideas come flowing out, like water through an opened sluice.

Chapter Fifteen

The month of January froze the landscape almost to a standstill. Some days Jem would have willingly remained at home, working in the moist-warmth of the cowshed, or taking care of chores around the yard, where he was in easy reach of the farmhouse and hot soup. However, he knew it was essential that he met Matt as often as possible, to receive instruction, and so he ventured out.

On the 21st of the month he crossed a field with iron-ridged furrows to meet his new young friend by the ditch on the far side. This was the day on which he was to be given a tour of the sluices and to be shown the network of channels that led to and from these watergates.

He had seen them all before, of course, during the years in which he had been growing up near the water meadows, but now he had to take note of them. It is one thing to be vaguely aware of some vast maze of waterways: it is quite another to *understand* it. Those ditches and drainage channels he had taken for granted as a young boy, had sailed his paper boats in and used as rivers and brooks when playing games like Robin Hood. Those dams and breaks at which he might have glanced occasionally on his way home from school. These all suddenly came into sharp focus. He saw them as he had never seen them before. And their complexity, their junctions, their side-channels and tributaries, their slopes and rises, their mudvalves and plugs, diverters and washes: all these had to be committed to memory.

'Well,' said Jem, as they stood on top of St Catherine's Hill and surveyed the meadows and their waterways with a sinking feeling in his stomach, 'where do we start?'

Matt took a slim white hand out of his right pocket and pointed to a corner of the complex system.

'We'll start over there, by them willows,' he said, his breath coming as bouquets of steam, 'and work our way round the edge. Once we've been all round it, then we start moving in to the middle ...'

'Sounds fine to me,' said Jem, blowing warm air on to his frozen fingers, 'so long as we can keep walkin' around. It's too cold to stand still for over long.'

'That's true,' replied Matt, but he did not look as if the cold were affecting him at all. He was not shivering and stamping around like Jem. He simply stood there, his hands in his great coat pockets, probably for somewhere to keep them. If they ever emerged they were like two delicate creatures, fluttering around the lamp of his face, indicating that Jem should take note of this or that when considering the drowning.

Once, Jem reached out and grasped his companion's hand, instinctively, as one would snatch at a moth that was bothering one's face, and found that the fingers were icy cold.

'You need some good mittens,' remarked Jem, after Matt had pulled his hand away. 'I'll get my mum to make you some from an old horse blanket.'

'Thank you,' said Matt, but he hardly looked concerned.

They began the tour of the water meadows, starting with the perimeter and then working their way inwards. It took a whole day just to locate all the sluices. They had no time to explore the system completely.

They met every day for six weeks after that.

At first Jem thought he would never understand a quarter of what he was supposed to, and he would toss and turn in his bed at night, moaning and groaning, obsessed with trying to remember *everything* the first time he was told. The other brothers who shared his bed and blankets complained to their mother that Jem was having bad dreams and keeping them all awake.

The two boys walked the fields, always together, exchanging gestures. Jem broke out of his earlier despondency, as one or two things began falling into place. Then a whole section of the meadows became comprehensible to him. This made him feel quite clever and special, in the way that learning something difficult often does. He felt privileged, knowing these were revelations to which only one other human being, on the whole face of the planet, was privy.

These were the secrets of the waterlands, these were the unravellings of the codes of earth and sky. Cryptic landscapes were offering their keys to him, uncovering their intricate parts to his gaze, disclosing their knitted natures.

Jem was like a watchmaker or a locksmith, finding his way through patterns of works, webs of parts, that touched at fine points in their dealings with the whole.

Over the next six weeks he came to know Matt Timbrell as a good young man, patient in his teachings. Jem had never before admired someone younger than himself, but he had to admit that he felt great admiration for Matt. Friendship too. Jem had never really had another friend, except Bess, and she was hardly ever around, always travelling to some part of the country, some far region which meant nothing to Jem.

'You'm a good lad, Matt,' said Jem one day, as they had just finished one of their innumerable tours. 'Once I said we had no room at the farm, but I'm going to ask on my father if you can come live with us. You must be tired o' that old shepherd's place by now.'

'No, Jem. You mustn't tell nobody about me. I'm feared of what will happen.'

Jem nodded, sitting down on the exposed root of a great oak that stood alone on a knoll.

'I forgot that,' he said. 'Still, you won't go away as soon as you've finished the teaching of me, will you?'

'I'm afraid I must.'

Jem nodded. 'Your family be missing you.'

'Yes.'

One thing that puzzled him was that he and Matt were so often together that they must have been seen by others. Yet no one had mentioned seeing Jem in the constant company of a stranger to the district. One or two people had said they had noticed Jem 'walking the fields' but there was no indication that Matt had been seen with him. He had no answer to this.

'Your education needs completing, Jem. February will soon be over and March will be on us.'

'I know,' said Jem, looking up into the dark eyes of his friend. 'I almost got the hang of that west section now. It all comes clearer each passin' day.'

'We must hope and pray it works.'

Jem studied the pale features of Matt Timbrell, shocked at the idea that after all this, the drowning might not be a success.

'Why won't it work?' he said. 'You learned it from your father John Timbrell.'

Matt blurted, 'But I never did try it myself, Jem. You got to remember that. I never once did get to *do* it. It's all school stuff with me. None of it practice. Like learning of places like France and Italy, but never goin' there. Like learning how to build a house, but never putting two bricks together. You see what I'm speakin' of?'

Jem said that he did.

'So,' repeated Matt, 'we got to pray as well, that it all works when you do it practical.'

To Jem this thought just added to the terrible weight of responsibility he felt towards the drowners. They would be relying on his skills to survive. There would be no second chance, because if the drowning were not successful this year, the tenant farmers would go under. They would drown all right, but in debts. The banks would foreclose on the mortgages and Sir Francis would triumph. It was a ghastly thought.

All this, on Jem's shoulders. Suddenly he didn't want it any more. It was too much for one youth, to expect him to bear such responsibility, such blame if it all went wrong. It was a job for a man full-grown, someone with a stronger will than Jem's.

'I can't do it,' he said, with a gasp. 'I can't do all this. Choose somebody else. Why me? Why not an older man, like my father?'

Matt said, 'It has to be you. You're the one what asked for me, Jem.'

Jem was indignant.

'I asked for you? Me? I never did.'

Matt nodded.

'Three times, you did. Three times.'

Jem shook his head, furiously, denying such a call.

'Jem, Jem, I don't want to fright you, but I couldn't have come if you didn't call, not for this. I come up from the river, because you wisht it ...'

'Yes, that river in Norfolk, but it weren't me that asked, it were James Halliwell.'

'No, *you*. Three times you wisht it, and here I be, standing before you, ready to do the work my father taught me. Think about this, but when you do, don't be feared of me, Jem, because I would do you no harm. Not ever. I'm going now.'

Matt turned and walked across the bleak fields, the trees seeming to move close to him, parentally, watching over him. The valleys narrowed, the hard earth folded round him, the whole landscape seemed supportive, protective of the light pale figure that walked upon it.

Jem stood on the same spot for a long time, the iron hoops of winter tightening round his chest. There was something he had been told, something he did not want to know. Matt had spoken obliquely, yet the meaning was plain.

'I called for Tom to come back,' he said to himself. 'I wisht him back three times, but Matt has come instead. It's something I don't want to look close on, not yet, not until I have to, and then maybe it'll have gone away and I won't need to at all.'

He made his way back to the farm, anxious to be indoors before the darkening sky turned to night.

Chapter Sixteen

Wesley Wickerman knew there was something going on. He could smell hope, other people's hope, like pollen in the air. There was nothing specific, nothing he could point to, but it was there just the same, an atmosphere, a feeling, the coming of spring.

Yet he also knew, instinctively, that it was not *his* spring that was promised. It was something to do with the drowners and farmers, and more particularly, with Jack Riley – the one the locals called Whoffer – and a boy, Jem Blunden. These two he had seen walking together lately, wearing the looks of conspirators.

Wickerman would have been suspicious if they had just been playing draughts together. What would a boy of fifteen and an old man of seventy-odd want in each other's company? It was an unnatural relationship. Jem Blunden was a serious young lad and Whoffer Riley a cantankerous half-timbered Ancient-of-Days. The two of them just did not fit together.

Wickerman hired a horse one morning, from The Green Man Inn, and took the road that led by the water meadows. Sure enough, the boy Jem was in a ditch by one of the sluices. He seemed to be alone, though it was difficult to tell, because just his shoulders and head were visible above the dyke. If anyone was with him, that person was smaller, and hidden from sight.

There had been a light fall of snow during the night, and when Wickerman looked down, he could see two sets of footprints leading to the ditch in which Jem Blunden was standing. The prints were all roughly of the same size.

One of his brothers, perhaps? thought Wickerman. Not Riley, anyway. The prints were too small for Riley, and in any case, there were no stump marks.

Wickerman wondered whether to go and confront the boys, but then changed his mind. There was another horseman coming up from the south and it appeared to be James Halliwell. Wickerman cursed, and turned his mount around, to take the road to Sir Francis Alderton's manor house.

'There's somethin' going on,' he told Sir Francis, when he arrived, 'and I aim to find out what it is.'

'That's what I hire you for,' said the aristocrat, taking a pinch of thick snuff from a red lacquer-wood box with a silver lid, and inhaling it with two loud snorts. 'Get in amongst 'em and discover what they're up to.'

'They're no doubt fussing over the next drowning,' said Wickerman. 'Worrying the devil out of those fields, wondering what to do.'

Sir Francis Alderton smiled thinly.

'That would be my guess, also. Still, there's no point in leaving them to their calculations, however futile such an exercise might be. Harass them. Make their miserable lives that much more miserable. Keep them spinning like tops.'

'Yes, sir,' muttered Wickerman. 'That I'll do.'

He rode back to the inn and returned the horse to the stables. There he had a pot of gin, some green fish, and contemplated his next move.

He decided that the boy Jem Blunden was relatively unimportant. What needed doing was to intimidate one of the drowners. It would have to be Riley. There would be very little problem in provoking a fight with the old man, who would swing his willow-stump at anyone who so much as mildly insulted him. In fact, challenges and threats to his dignity formed in the air around Whoffer Riley's head, like pixies out of marsh mist. You didn't even need to voice an insult. All you had to do was look at the old man askance, and he would stick out his chin and growl, 'Seen yer fill, have ye?'

That evening Wickerman went to The Royal Oak, where he knew Whoffer Riley would be holding forth to his cronies. When he stepped through the door, Wickerman was immediately aware of a change of atmosphere in the room. All talk suddenly dropped to a near whisper. Men's eyes, once having seen who had come through the door, deliberately avoided the latest arrival.

Wickerman smiled to himself. He enjoyed his notoriety.

The landlord came over to him wearing a surly look on his face, which bothered Wickerman not in the least.

'A jug of ale,' ordered Wickerman, 'and some bread and cheese.'

'I want no trouble in here,' stated the landlord, flatly.

'You won't get none from me,' replied Wickerman, 'but I can't promise for them.'

He nodded contemptuously at Whoffer Riley's group, standing around a barrel by the fire.

The landlord's hard eyes never left Wickerman's face.

'No trouble,' he repeated. 'I don't care who starts it. If there is some, it'll be because you came here. You understand? Before I wed the landlady of this here inn, I was a naval man. You see this?' He tapped a long hard object stuck in his belt, under his shirt. He leaned forward over Wickerman. 'A marlinspike. As a bosun, I used to lay out drunken sailors cold. I can do the same with any man, be he mariner or no.'

'Just make sure I'm as drunk as those sailors before you try that one on me,' snarled Wickerman. 'Sober you wouldn't find me standing waiting for the blow.'

'I merely make the warning,' said the landlord, 'so's you know where you are.'

Once the kitchen girl had brought him his ale and food, Wickerman leaned back and studied the group around the barrel. Their talk was subdued now that he had entered the room, but it was still obvious that a meeting was going on, and Wickerman intended to find out what it was, this very night.

Wickerman stayed until Whoffer Riley left the inn, and then he followed the old man outside. Riley had borrowed a lighted lamp from the stables and was taking the path down to the Itchen by the time Wickerman caught sight of him. Wickerman himself lit no lamps. He followed behind, the soles of his shoes crunching softly on the frosty ground.

Ahead of him, Riley's lamp was swinging back and forth, as the old man swayed as violently as a ship in a storm. This was not because he had drunk too much ale, but because his willow leg caused him to lurch slightly with every forward step using that limb.

It was an awkward object for one thing.

When Whoffer Riley had replaced his right leg with a lump of wood, he chose something stout and hardy, larger in girth than the flesh and bone it had supplanted. Whoffer had stated that he wanted no 'sticks' in place of his arm and leg, 'loike a blamed scarecrow moight have!' but good solid logs, that would stand a hammering on the hard chalk of Hampshire.

'I bain't no crow scarer,' he had said at the time. 'I be a *man* and a blamed foine one at that, though I say so meself. Crack willer is what oi'll be having, *cleft* – not sawn – from the trunk, loike a good cricket bat, then seasoned and shaped the same. Her won't warp then, and will stand no end of battering and bashing, same as a bat, see, and never a split in her.

'Weathers well too, do willer. Look at garden trugs, made of the selfsame wood. Last forever, they do, out in the wind and the rain, snow and hail ...'

So Wickerman followed the man with cricket bats for arm and leg, until he reached the Itchen and started clumping across the bridge that spanned its rushing waters.

Wickerman made a noise and Whoffer Riley turned, peering back, holding his lamp at arm's length away from his face so that he could better see into the darkness.

'Who's there?' called the old man. 'Come forrard.'

Wickerman stepped into the pool of light thrown by the lantern.

'It's me, you old fool, Wesley Wickerman.'

Whoffer Riley glowered.

'Don't be callin' me an ole fool, ye snip!'

Wickerman snorted contemptuously.

'I'll call you what I like, and you'll take it, Riley. You can huff and puff for the benefit of your friends at the inn, but it don't wash with me. You're all wind, old man, and a few bits of wood. Nothing else left of you worth mentioning.'

'Ye ... damn ye,' cried the old man, swinging his artificial limb at Wickerman's head.

The hired man caught the wooden arm, firmly in his meaty hand. He stopped it dead. He held it there, still as a rock, while Whoffer Riley strained against his far greater strength, going red in the face and spluttering like a half-blocked drain in a rainstorm.

'It's no good, old man. Give it up. Remember. You threw the first blow, not me. I just talked, and you went to violence on me.' He gripped the old man by the throat and forced him back against the parapet of the bridge, so that his spine was arched over the waters of the Itchen.

The lamp fell from Whoffer's three good fingers, and splashed, sizzling, in the tumbling waters below. It was swept away on the flood like a small boat.

Blackness engulfed the two men.

'Now, what's going on between you and the boy, that Jem Blunden? Tell me or I'll break your neck like a twig.'

'Nuthin',' spluttered Whoffer, struggling to grip his opponent with his half-hand. 'Nuthin' goin' on. Don't let me go,' his eyes were wild and round, 'oi can't swim.'

'That a fact, is it?' smiled Wickerman. 'Afraid of the water, are you? Tell me what I want and I'll let you up, but if you hold back, why then I'll just take my hands away quick and you'll float like a feather down to that there freezing river.'

'Oi – don't – know – nuthin' ...'

'Liar!'

They remained locked together for the next several minutes with Wickerman trying to force the old man to give him the information he wanted. Finally, he realised that Riley would never talk to him, no matter how much pain he inflicted. It seemed to him that Riley was a keystone in the whole conspiracy, so it might well crumble without him. To get rid of Riley might serve his purpose just as well.

Whoffer Riley was grunting, 'Let – go – on – me!'

'Remember,' smiled Wickerman, 'I didn't push you over the edge of the bridge. I simply did as you asked me. I let you go ...'

With that, he released his hold on the old man who fell backwards into the night. There was a sound as he hit the surface of the river down below, but it was too dark for Wickerman to see.

'*Bon voyage*,' he called down, and then made his way back to the inn to find a lamp and chase away the blackness.

Chapter Seventeen

It was true that Whoffer Riley could not swim, but he knew he could not sink either. The wooden arm and leg, one at each opposite corner, would have kept him afloat forever and day. He had known this, before Wickerman let him drop into the river, because he took his baths in the river during the summer months, and had once or twice lost his footing. He bobbed like a cork on the surface, hardly any of him below the waterline.

He lay on his back and allowed the flood to carry him downstream to some shallows where he struggled ashore. Although he had not drowned, as Wickerman had expected, Whoffer was terribly cold. The waters of the Itchen were freezing and if he did not get warm soon he knew he could collapse and die from exposure.

Whoffer staggered across country, the cold wind sinking icy blades into his vulnerable husk. His old cough, the one that tore his chest apart as if it were paper, returned to visit him as it did on occasion.

Once, he fell amongst the frosted ferns, and lay there thinking it might be nice just to go to sleep, but in the back of his brain he knew that to do so would be fatal. He struggled upright on to his good leg, dragging the willow-stump after it, until he was propped and ready for another onslaught against the dark landscape before him.

'If'n oi stand still overlong,' he grunted to himself, 'this ole willer will think she's been watered and planted on purpose, loike a cuttin', and take root here and now, and then where will oi be? Sproutin' green with the new spring, instead of working the meadows with that whippersnapper Jem Blunden ...'

In this way, chattering to himself to keep him from falling down from exhaustion and fatigue, he kept going. Around him, the black countryside moved with night creatures: owls, foxes, bats. These were the shadow beings, seldom seen, but out in their dozens during the dark hours. Normally, Whoffer was aware of such creatures. He had lived in the country all his life, and he was almost one of them. Tonight, however, his mind was out of its head, and he did not know them.

About half a mile from the Blunden farm, just when he felt he had to drop, Whoffer came across a huge compost heap, in which silage had been mixed with dung. The mound was chilled on the outside, but he broke the crust to find it had a heart of moist heat. Such rotting piles create their own warmth from fermenting vegetation at their core.

Whoffer ignored the smell, dropped into the fibrous mess, and lay there with steam rising around him. After a while he could feel the heat warming through his skin to his cold bones. It crept over him, until he felt sure the flesh and bone part of him had thrown off the numbness of approaching death.

He must have slept a little, because he woke up with a start. The compost had cooled around him, and he struggled to stand upright. It was still very dark, but he knew the countryside well and was sure he was on the road to the Blunden farm.

Once again he dragged himself forward, his bones beginning to chill. He concentrated on his good leg, pivoting on the willow stump, to land down hard on the single remaining appendage which still owned all its digits. It was a slow business, but he was encouraged by the snuffling of the dairy cows in their stalls. If he was close enough to hear them, he was almost at the farm.

Then suddenly, he was up against the farmhouse door, and he let out a thankful sigh. He tried knocking with his three knuckles, but it was a feeble sound that came out of it, so he felt around the step in the darkness and found a bootscraper. He used this to hammer on the door.

There were noises within. A few moments later a lamp was lit, the light showing beneath the door. Then a voice called out, 'Who's there?'

'It's me,' gasped Whoffer. 'Jack Riley.'

'That you, Whoffer?' cried a surprised Alex Blunden.

'Yes, yes. Oi be freezin' to death out here. Open the door, for pity's sake.'

There were the sounds of heavy bolts being drawn, then the door was flung back. Something, hanging on the hook on the inside of the door, swung out and struck Whoffer in the face, almost knocking him over. It was a hare, left there to decay, until it was rotten enough to be jugged.

Alex Blunden, screwed up his face and held his nose.

'By God, you stinks, man!'

'Can't help that,' said Whoffer. 'That there dung 'eap saved me britches. Would've froze to death wi'out it.'

'And look at the missis's step!' cried Alex, holding the lamp higher aloft. 'She'll murder someone, over that mess, so she will. It were scrubbed white as an angel's wing not six hours since.'

Whoffer Riley's teeth were chattering.

'Be ye goin' to let me pass, or no?' he growled indignantly. 'For oi be turnin' to a block on ice here afore yer very eyes, so oi be.'

Alex stepped back into the scullery and let Whoffer enter, shaking his head at the green fluid and bits of silage that dripped from Whoffer's clothes on to the clean floor. Dorothy Riley came into the scullery with a mop-hat on and a blanket-coat around her. She looked at the floor, then at Whoffer Riley: a thin, brittle man, quivering before her.

Alex was looking at her with a wary expression, waiting for the storm.

'Get him into the parlour, Alex, you great lummock,' she said finally. 'Stoke up the embers on the fire. The man's freezing.'

They got the fire going between them and stuck Whoffer in front of it, wrapping a thick blanket around him. Dorothy put a kettle on the flames, once they were good and high. Whoffer sat staring at the faggots as they hissed out blue-green flames.

'What happened?' asked Dorothy.

'Oi be sorry 'bout the floor,' said Whoffer, 'it bein' so clean an' all.'

'Niver mind the floor,' snapped Dorothy. 'Tell us what happened.'

'Oi fell off the bridge.'

The farmer and his wife stared at him, then Alex said, 'there must be more to it than that, Whoffer Riley.'

The old man nodded.

'Got into an argument with that there Wickerman. Oi let fly at him, on the bridge. We had oursen's a struggle, and over oi topples.' He knocked his wooden arm against his wooden leg. 'Me bits o' tree saved me from sinking. Then the dung 'eap – beggin' yer floor's pardon, missis – warmed me through, just as oi were sayin' goodbye to the owls and farewell to the weasels. Comes of havin' a temper, oi suppose.'

'What was you argying about?' asked Alex.

Whoffer Riley looked up, into his friend's eyes.

'He's on to us.'

'On to *what*, man? Make some sense.'

'On to me and young Jem. We got it calculated – the drownin'. Jem's been walkin' the meadows, all winter, calculatin' in that head o' his, about the drownin'. He come to me thon other day and says, "Whoffer, ye must help me tell the drowners and farmers what to do. They won't believe a spit of a boy, but take it from me, oi knows what's what." An' I believe he do, Alex. I believe he do.'

There was a sound from the doorway, and all three heads turned to see Jem standing there.

'Jem?' said his father. 'What's this?'

''Tis true, Dad,' he said. 'I were out in the fields, just nearing February, when I felt a power come over me. Maybe it was the power of the Lord, but twern't the Devil, that's for sure because it were for the good, not for the bad. Anyways, I knowed that if I studied the meadows hard, it would come to me how to do the drowning. And so it has. I been out there

110

every day for the last six or seven weeks, Dad, studying them 'til my eyes was sore. I think I can do it ...'

'You *think*? Boy, this has got to be done right, this one time, or we'm all finished.'

Jem said quietly, 'Nobody can be *sure*, Dad. Even when John Timbrell were with us, he were never *sure*. One thing be certain, I knows more than any man alive. It's me, or nothing.'

'We've still got many good drowners. Men what have worked the sluices for years ...'

Dorothy interrupted him.

'Worked the sluices, Alex, but that just means opening and closing some wooden gates.'

'Missis is roight,' remarked Whoffer. 'We need a *plan*, some sort of scheme. It bain't goin' to work wi' out one.'

'Mightn't work *with* one,' said Alex.

'Better than nothin',' persisted Whoffer, 'an' surely Wickerman thinks so too, for he took hisself out to put me in the grave this very night, thinkin' oi was the master brain a-hind it all.'

'He tried to kill you?'

'Let's say he worked the situayshun, so to speak. He throws up a challenge, and oi, like the fool oi be, takes him up on it. Oi got no proof that Wickerman were out to murder, but he were baitin' me into letting fly with this 'ere left bat. He catches it, firm and strong, in that boxer's hand of his. We struggles on the bridge and then he lets go, an' oi falls into the water.'

Alex said, 'We could still ...'

'Let's beat him on the meadows, Dad,' said Jem. 'If'n the constables took him away, he'd be back again quick as an adder, with Sir Francis's help. Let's get rid on him, by doing the drowning, proper.'

Dorothy caught her husband's eye and nodded firmly.

Alex sighed.

'You'm ganging up on me.'

So it was settled, amongst them. Alex and Whoffer would persuade the farmers and drowners that Jem should oversee the drowning. They would not call him the Master Drowner, not yet, not until a successful drowning had been achieved. It was not going to be an easy task, in any case, getting the others to agree. There would be the stubborn ones, who would prefer a random sluice opening to following the instructions of a youth who had no prior knowledge of the greater task.

Chapter Eighteen

Alex Blunden left the farmhouse that very hour, to go round to all the drowners in the district. He set up a meeting for six o'clock the following morning. There he hoped to persuade the drowners that the annual drowning should take place immediately, under the instructions of his son Jem. He would have Whoffer Riley to back him up.

It had to be done that day. Not only was the time right, but if they delayed Wickerman might find some way to stop them. The sluices would have to be padlocked after that, and guarded, to stop outsiders from tampering with the drowning. All it needed was someone to open a key sluice and all the work would be ruined.

On the way home, at four o'clock, Alex met an early rider. It was James Halliwell, exercising his mare, Sheba.

'Out early, Mr Halliwell?' remarked Alex.

'I could say the same of you, Blunden. You look like some character from a Shakespeare tragedy. Hugger-mugger, that's what you appear to be.'

'I don't know what that means, I'm sure.'

James Halliwell patted the neck of his snorting mare.

'It means you look as if you're bearing dark secrets.'

Alex Blunden nodded.

'That's a fact, Mr Halliwell.'

James said, 'Well, keep 'em to yourself. You don't need to tell me, not unless it involves my help in some way. The less people know, the tighter the security.'

Alex was a little relieved. He had been planning on telling James Halliwell, if that man had asked what he was about, but he preferred to keep it all amongst the drowners. Their loyalty was unquestioned because they each had a stake in keeping the secret. Though James Halliwell was in no way suspected of being an enemy, he was still an outsider, and once you made an exception the secret became a loose thing, a wild creature.

'Thank you, Mr Halliwell, I'm glad for that.'

'Well, judging from your expression, it's a project of utmost importance to you. Good luck with it, whatever it is, and call on me if you need assistance.'

With that the horseman took off across the pasture, his mount throwing divots at the sky.

The drowners gathered near the river, close to the Hospital of St Cross, where Alex Blunden and Whoffer Riley explained to them what had occurred, and what they proposed the men should do about it. Jem himself stood to one side, and said nothing. This had been agreed beforehand. It was best to let the senior drowners argue it out amongst themselves. Jem was having enough trouble convincing *himself* that he was capable of managing the drowning, let alone try to persuade others of it.

As expected, there were several dissenters.

'What I don't understand,' said Davey Waxbender, 'is where young Jem got his skill from. I mean, John never told 'im, and John's long dead.'

'He says he has a feel for the work,' Alex answered. 'Some things come natural to a man.'

'Not master-drowning don't,' remarked another man. 'That's a skill has got to be learned, or we wouldn't need apprentices, would we?'

'True, true,' came several murmurs from the group.

Jem felt he ought to say something here.

'Young Tom give me some instruction,' he said, surprising even Whoffer and his father with the remark. 'He told me some of it and the rest I studied over the last two months.'

'Tom Timbrell was dead afore his father,' stated Davey.

'Nevertheless,' replied Jem, and left it at that.

The arguments swayed back and forth, no one really getting anywhere, until finally Whoffer Riley stamped his stump, drumming on the cold ground, calling for attention, and said, 'Roight, all those what agree to let Jem Blunden do the drownin', stand off over there.'

A number of men moved to the spot indicated, leaving about a third of the drowners.

'Roight!' snapped Whoffer. 'Them as be left, pay attention. What one of ye *will* do the master-drownin' then? Come on, step forward. It's got to be done today, not tomorrer. Let's 'ave a volunteer. I'll go with the man, whoever he be. If he's brave enough to master the drownin', then I'm a-hind him all the way. Let's have yer then! Step out.'

Not a man amongst them moved, except to shuffle his feet.

Whoffer looked up towards the heavens.

'Them old grey clouds up there, they looks to be about to chuck a bit o' rain down. And the river be swole this mornin' loike a torrent. And the frost be deep and sharp today ... but who amongst ye can read the signs? Come on, there must be one, ye've all be argyin' against young Jem. Meself, oi'd soon as face the Frenchie cannons again, or cavalry swishin' the air with them bent swords they call sabres, rather than do the master drownin', but then oi'm not as brave as some. What man, oi say? Let's see his face. Oi'll pin a medal on it meself.'

Davey Waxbender broke the silence.

'All right,' he said sourly, 'you've made your point, Whoffer Riley. None of us knows a nounce about the master drowning, and none of us dares try, so let's get to it.'

There was no time for savouring triumph. Jem led everyone to the river, where he stood on the bank and studied the rapids. The water was over the stepping stones, but not up to the curve of the arch on the bridge. Would it increase within the next few hours? He turned his attention to the skies. It certainly looked like rain, but the clouds were high and there was a strong overwind bending the tops of the firs. There had been snow up on the downs, but a general thaw was a long way off ...

For an hour Jem walked the water meadows, noting all the nuances of the weather and landscape, asking which fields were intended for pasture, and which for the plough. Finally, he took a deep swallow and began to issue his instructions: which sluices were to be opened and for how long; which of the water gates were to remain closed; the ditches that were to be diverted, and in which direction; the channels that should remain dammed and those that needed to be breached. He spoke with authority, feeling Matt's confidence within him, and the men moved out, on to the flatlands, the waterlands, to do his bidding. No more voices were raised in dissent. Once the Master Drowner's plan was in action, all knew that to delay any part of it might result in overall failure.

Gates were opened, blockages removed. River water began swilling between narrow banks, on its annual series of journeys along the canals – rushing, tumbling, swirling around corners. A weak winter sun came out to sparkle on the lines of water that streaked down their channels, searching for an outlet. The quicksilver of the farmlands had been let loose, to work its magic.

There was a gush, a high cascade, as the first of the torrents hit an end barrier and began flooding into the top meadow, spreading silently across the frozen ground. Then the second wave slammed into its dam, and turned at right angles, east and west, to form a counterflood. It was a race between the two lakes, as to which of them reached the centre field first. They each sent out rays, horns of water, which curled around the edge in an effort to outflank the other.

Where they met, they mingled, becoming one, all competition between them having melted with touch. No longer rivals, they were closer than allies, they were a single army.

The flood finally reached the first of the terraces, slid smoothly over the edge, began its conquest of the meadow below the high ground.

All over the area, similar actions were in progress, as men wound winches, turned wheels, swung handles and removed the sluice gates that had held back the waters of the Itchen for the past year. The river, freed from its bondage, flowed joyously along its artificial pathways, to open land.

Amongst all this feverish activity, Jem walked, his brow furrowed, his voice issuing last-minute orders, as he noted the flow of the river water on to the precious pastureland.

By evening it was all over. The sluices had been closed. The water lay profoundly still and calm in the meadows. The landscape had become a huge mirror, reflecting the pale lilac of a sky drifting into sleep. A single frosted star was imperceptibly climbing across the heavens, its track mimicked by a ghostly twin in the waters below St Catherine's Hill.

The drowners were gathered there, on the crest of the hill, looking down on their work. They had recreated God's great biblical flood in miniature. They had controlled the waters of Babylon, they were the lords of the Tigris and Euphrates, the masters of Mesopotamia. They had borrowed the waters of the Jordan, and had stolen the White and Blue Niles for their own purposes.

The shallow waters, warmer than the earth in winter, would bring on the fresh spring grass, at least six weeks before Sir Francis could find good pastureland for *his* cattle.

'It *worked*,' said Jem, in a voice clogged with emotion.

'Aye,' agreed Whoffer Riley, 'it worked as good as ever John Timbrell made it work. Yer a little wonder, Jem.'

'Not me,' said Jem emphatically. 'I just learned what to do.'

Alex put his arm around his son's shoulders.

'Well, you learned good, son. You'm our new Master Drowner.'

There was a murmuring of assent from the men who were still standing in an awed group, staring at their day's work, knowing that they had been saved from eviction, perhaps from starvation. There was still much to do. There were still things that could go wrong. The beef was not yet in the market square. The butter and milk not yet on the stalls. But the main battle was over. They could tackle the rest as it came.

The men began to drift away, in twos and threes, some of them bound for home, others to be posted as sentries over the day's work. The sluices had already been secured with massive iron locks, but there was the chance that someone might attempt to smash through one of them with an axe.

Jem and his father were the last to leave. Jem was still entranced by his own handiwork but was in no danger of becoming swollen headed. He knew he had been just a tool. The real Master Drowner was living out in a shepherd's hut. Jem decided to pay him a visit to tell him the good news.

Chapter Nineteen

Jem called first at The Green Man Inn, to see if Matt was there, cleaning boots. When he spoke to the landlady, however, she denied all knowledge of Matt.

'An't no lad of that name 'ere. All my boots are live-in lads. I don't hire no part-timers,' she said, shaking her head.

Jem said, 'Maybe someone else hired him. The landlord, perhaps? Maybe just for a few days or so?'

The landlady folded her arms under her bosom.

'I does all the hirin' and such, and I never hired no boy called Matt, nor any lads for that matter, not in two years.'

'Thank you, ma'am,' said Jem. 'I'll be on my way.'

Darkness was upon the land and Jem hired a lantern from the inn and set off along the track lined with the ruts of wagon wheels, for the shepherd's hut once described to him by Matt. When he reached the downs, he took a narrow path out into the fields, his feet feeling the flints through the soles of his boots.

Out on the chalk downs, Jem was beginning to wish he had left his task until the morning. There was a weak moon out, now, but it barely shone with enough light to see the white path by. He concentrated on the sound of his own footfalls, to give him something to take his mind off his surroundings.

Finally, he found himself outside the shepherd's hut, where Matt was supposed to be living. There was a terrible smell, coming from somewhere nearby, and Jem gagged for a while, hoping to get used to the stink before searching the hut. After a while he could take his hand from his nose without feeling as if he was going to be sick. The odour remained in the air, but Jem was able to ignore it enough to continue with his quest.

He approached the drystone walls of the hut. A chill wind was sweeping over the downs, following the smooth, rounded feminine hills, sliding down into the hollows. Jem buttoned his coat at the collar, and stared at the ramshackle dwelling.

The place looked silent, eerie, in the moonlight. Jem still had his lamp lit and he held it up as he approached the open doorway.

'Hello?' he called. 'Be you there, Matt?'

There was no reply to this request. Jem nodded his head in grim satisfaction. He had come to the hut to find out for himself whether his suspicions had any grounding in fact. Now that he was here, he was almost certain. The hut had not been lived in for a long time, that much at least was sure. He held the lamp higher.

'Why, there's no roof on it,' he said to himself.

Jem advanced to the door and held the lamp just inside. He stuck his head in after it. The beams of the lantern danced around the tight little walls inside the shepherd's hut, rousting the shadows out of the corners. Light flickered on old cobwebs, covered in chalk dust. There was a dirt floor covered in sheeps' droppings, with not a footprint to be seen. The place had not been disturbed for many months, except by animals seeking temporary shelter from bad weather.

'So,' muttered Jem.

He withdrew from the doorway and began looking around the outside, to see if there was a bivouac against the walls. The stench from the grasses nearby was appalling and he decided to make his stay as brief as possible.

He stepped out, off the path, and immediately his leg went from under him.

'Whaa ...!' he cried, falling to one side.

The lamp went spinning out his grasp and disappeared in front of his eyes, as if it had been swallowed by the darkness. A distant *thump* followed, from somewhere down below. Jem reached out and carefully felt around his feet, until he pushed his hand into space. There was a deep hole there, amongst the ferns, and his lamp was at its bottom.

'That'll cost me,' he grumbled.

He felt around a little more, to see if the lantern could be recovered, but the hole – which indeed appeared to be the source of the awful stench that was bothering him so much – was too large and apparently too deep to even think of trying to recover his lost property. In any event, it was probably broken beyond repair. There was nothing for it but to ask his father to replace the hired lamp. After the successful drowning that day, Jem did not believe his father would be too churlish with him.

'An accident, after all ...' he said to himself.

The cold wind increased in strength, and Jem decided it was time to be going home. He started on along the path, towards the main track, but stopped suddenly, and looked behind him.

'Who's there?' he called.

He had heard a sound, in the bracken, by the hole.

There was no answer.

'I heard you,' cried Jem, now thoroughly frightened. 'Is that you, Matt?'

The crisp bracken crackled and Jem tried again.

'Bess, is that you, home from your travels? Did you follow me out here?'

No reply.

'All right,' cried Jem, 'you'm scarin' me. Do that make you satisfied – I admit, I'm frit,' he added, using an old schoolboy rhyme.

Suddenly a white shape emerged from the bracken and Jem screamed, 'Stay away from me! Stay away ...'

He backed away, only to be stopped by a wall. The shape bounded off a few metres on hearing the scream, but turned to face him once he had gone quiet. Now that it was out in the open, he could see what it was, a lost sheep. The animal had probably been looking for the shepherd's hut, to get out of the biting wind, and had been disturbed by Jem's scent.

'Oh, I knew *that*,' said Jem, in relief. 'I knew you was a sheep, the whole time.'

Still, his heart was racing fast, and he wasted no time in

getting to the main track and finding his way back to Winchester. When he arrived there, he called in at the inn and told them of his accident. The landlady was a little gruff, but Jem told her he would replace the lantern in the morning. She seemed satisfied.

Jem then made his way back to the farm, sure in his mind that the boy Matt was what Jem thought him to be. The strange thing was, it did not scare him. He knew Matt would do him no harm and, now that the drowning was over, there might be something that Jem could do for Matt.

When he reached the farmhouse, he found someone waiting for him outside. Two someones, in fact. Bess and her lurcher Meg. They looked pleased to see him. He was glad too, not only that Bess had come back to him but because he wanted to ask her something very important, something that only folk close to the supernatural might be able to answer.

Gypsies were folk like that.

Chapter Twenty

Wesley Wickerman stood on St Catherine's Hill and looked down on the water meadows below him. The scene that lay below him was serene, a patchwork of geometrical lakes amongst which men moved, tending to small tasks at the heads of artificial streams. It was a scene which might have inspired a poet to write something on tranquillity, but in Wickerman's heart there was nothing but turmoil.

'Blast their eyes!' he growled, slapping his hickory stick against his thigh. 'How did they get that done? Not by accident, that's a fact.'

He went from the hill, down to St Cross, and asked one of the brothers in red to find the Master for him.

Master North sent a message that he could be seen in his study, and Wickerman was led there.

'Well?' asked the robed Master of St Cross. 'What brings you here, Wickerman? A message from Alderton?'

Wickerman regarded North with some distaste. He did not like men who pretended to be scholars and clergymen, who raped the institutions of which they were put in charge, and made themselves rich on it. It was not that Wickerman disapproved of wealth, even wealth gained by exploiting the poor, but that such a thing should be done with impunity.

He was, in fact, jealous. He was incensed by the fact that you had to be an educated man to make yourself rich by stealing from others, and remain safe from prison.

The Master of St Cross had done nothing against the law of the land, and everything against the laws of God. His actions might be those of a tyrant, milking his subjects dry, but he could not be termed a thief, embezzler, or a fraud, though in truth he was all those things, and more. He simply took and used money which had been placed in his trust, for his own hedonistic purposes. Wickerman despised a man who would never have to face the consequences of his deeds, at least not in this world. A man who hid behind vague wordings of old parchments, like a child hiding behind the skirts of his nurse.

Master North was a thoroughly immoral man who had done nothing illegal.

'No, no message,' said Wickerman. 'I come to ask you if you saw the drowners at work yesterday.'

North nodded, pushing his hands into his sleeves to keep them warm. Wickerman noticed an open bible on a stand near to the fireplace and added the word 'hypocrite' to the list of reasons why he loathed Master North.

'Yes, I saw them, but it was too late to get word to Alderton. I sent a rider this morning. Surely there's no problem? They were being directed by a youth, a mere boy of fourteen or so. Jack Riley was there too, at the centre of things. I imagined the result would be like last year, a fiasco of overflooding and underwatering.'

Wickerman was a little taken aback. Jack Riley? So the old buzzard had not drowned in the Itchen that night? Riley was like a cat with nine lives. Nothing to be done about it now, however, except make denials if Riley was ready to accuse him of attempted murder. Better to concentrate on the matter in hand: the flooding of the meadows.

'It looks very much like they've been successful,' growled Wickerman. 'Them fields out there have about six inches of water in them, over all. Not one of 'em ruined, to my sight. What did this boy look like?'

North described the youth and Wickerman nodded his head thoughtfully.

'I know the tyke. Alex Blunden's son. Stared me out once, on the road, as he passed by on a wagon, but I gave him more back that he could put out.'

'Well, all I can tell you is that he appeared to be the instigator. They followed him around as if he were Jesus the

124

Nazarene, and he waving his hands, this way and that, while his disciples did his bidding.'

Wickerman thanked North for his information, knowing he would have to do something more positive now that his master knew of the drowning. There would be hell to pay when he next saw Sir Francis, and he wanted something to lay at the Baronet's feet. A peace offering. The death of the tyke might do nicely.

What was worrying Wickerman was where the boy had learned his craft. It was widely thought that the skills of the Master Drowner had died with John Timbrell. If that were so, had the boy just been lucky, or was there some secret source of information missed by himself and Sir Francis?

Wickerman had noticed that the boy often went walking near the chapel on St Catherine's Hill, at sunset. That would be the time to confront the youth, and present him with a choice: name his source or join Angel and the angels.

Something struck Wickerman as funny and his broad face, with its flat broken nose, took on an unusual expression.

It was a look of mirth.

Angel amongst the angels. That was worthy of a scholar. That was something Master North might have said. Angel Silke was amongst the silken angels. It just went to show that you didn't need an education to make twists and turns with words. All you needed was a sharp mind. He had that all right. A sharp mind – and a sharp sword. The two most important tools of the successful murderer. He had them both.

Chapter Twenty-one

The gloaming wrapped itself around the hill of St Catherine as Jem made his way to its summit to the chapel there. He was on his way to meet Matt and to talk with his friend for one last time, for Matt had indicated that once the drowning was over, he would be on his way back to his home.

He had rushed through his chores at the farm that afternoon, feeding the chickens and the pigs early, so that he could get out to the hill while the light was still in the sky. Now that he *knew* what Matt was, he thought he preferred the day, but standing on the hill, waiting, with the night coming in over the downs, it did not seem to matter after all.

Jem stood amongst some trees, as the light drained from the sky, and the deep dark of late winter days moved in to take its place. There was no wind, just a slight fluff of snow in the air, but nothing too serious. Nothing that would interfere with the drowning. It was not cold enough for that.

Someone came out of the trees, walking towards him, his pale face unsmiling, his black eyes strangely empty.

'Matt,' said Jem softly. 'You've come.'

'I can't stay long,' said the other boy. 'Just a short while. It's ... it's hard to be here. You wouldn't understand but it takes all my strength. I have to go home, I'm weak ...'

'Home?' said Jem. 'To the river, you mean?'

Matt looked at him and nodded, solemnly.

'I as much told you, last time we met.'

'That you were not really called Matt, but had been given another name – Tom, Tom Timbrell.'

The figure before Jem nodded again.

'That's true. I be Tom Timbrell. You wisht me back, three times, Jem Blunden, and I come to you. I feel weak now. My time be gone.'

'What I want to know,' said Jem, 'is how come nobody but me can see you?'

Tom nodded. 'Others can see me, Jem, if I let 'em. It's up to me. I'm the one what lets it happen.'

Jem started forward, then stopped.

'I wanted to say to you, Tom, how sorry I be now, that we was never friends,' he blurted out. 'I *wanted* to be your friend, but I was frit. You was always so much cleverer than me, and I was frit of being made a fool by you. That were foolish in itself, I see that now. But you be a ghost and I don't know if you understand.'

Tom's eyes were shining behind the emptiness now.

'I understand, Jem. I were scared too, of your strength. You was a big lad, and I thought maybe you would knock me about if I come up and held out my hand, so I never did. We was both a bit daft. A touch of the turnips in both of us, eh?'

Jem laughed, feeling good inside now, feeling warm and secure in the presence of this spirit of his old enemy. If you had told him this event would take place, sometime in his past, he would have started in dread, for there was not a boy alive who wished to meet a ghost. Now that he had one, within touching distance, all he felt was a great sorrow for what the ghost was missing, mixed with a great joy for having been able to unburden himself of his guilt over Tom's death.

'Tom,' said Jem, 'you saved us, you know that. Now I want to do something for you. I spoke with Bess last night about you. She said ghosts can only come back if they be stuck between earth and heaven, and can't find their way. Be that true, or no?'

'True,' said Tom.

'She said bein' a ghost, you can't tell me what to do, but I know what to do. If I find your body, where it's stuck, and have it buried in the grave they put down for you at the churchyard, your soul will find its path. True, or no?'

'True,' said Tom.

127

'So what you've got to do, Tom, is tell me where your body lies, and I'll see it's done.'

Tom looked distressed.

'I can't see it plain, but I know it's under a dark shadow, caught there in something made by man ...'

'Made by man? Is it a jetty, Tom? Or an old sunk boat? Is it wood?'

'It's very hard and cold.'

Jem said, 'Stone then. Not wood. A shadow you say? It must be a bridge then.'

Tom shook his head violently, his eyes were closed and he was in some kind of pain, trying to get Jem to say the words.

'Not a bridge,' Tom gasped. 'Not a bridge. Something else. Oh, say it, Jem, say it!'

Jem was in distress himself now. He wanted to see into Tom's mind, but he was not clever enough. Tom was the clever one. If they had been in each other's place, Tom would have got it in an instant. What else could it be? Something that spanned the river, that much was certain. Only bridges spanned rivers, surely. Lock gates? But they were made of wood. An iron sluice, perhaps?

He stared at Tom's pale face, powder white – powder white – white as powder – white as *flour* ...

'I have it!' he cried. 'It's a mill. One of them mills built over the river, so the water flows underneath the whole building. Am I right, Tom?'

Tom's face suddenly glowed.

Jem said, 'You'm stuck underneath, caught in the brickwork. That's it, eh, Tom? Well, we'll have you out of there in no time.'

'Thank you,' said Tom, softly.

They stood there, quietly regarding each other for a while, then Jem said, 'I have to go, Tom. I don't suppose we'll see each other again, will we?'

'No,' replied Tom. 'I don't suppose we will. Not around

here, anyways. Maybe somewhere else, you know, when you come and join me.'

'Well then,' said Jem, 'you won't mind me saying that I hope it's not for a long time yet.'

'I hope so too.'

Jem turned and began to walk down St Catherine's Hill, towards the water meadows. When he was some distance away, he turned and shouted, 'Goodbye. You saved our bacon. You surely did. Without you the drowning would have been a disaster. You did it all, really.'

When Jem was out of sight a man stepped out of the trees and advanced towards Tom. It was Wesley Wickerman and his face was set in a tight manner. He had heard Jem's final words, clearly.

'So,' said the hired man, 'it was you that did the master drowning, eh? I didn't think that Blunden boy could be responsible. He's all oak between his ears.'

Tom said, 'Jem's got more there than you think.'

Wickerman leaned his weight on his hickory stick.

'And what have we got here, then? Where did you spring from?'

'My father was John Timbrell.'

Wickerman nodded thoughtfully, his sharp blue eyes narrowing, their depth lost in the darkening of the sky behind the hill. He stood upright and clipped at a weed with his stick, taking its head clean off with one swipe.

'So, one of the Timbrell brats. That makes sense. Your father passed on something to you, did he? You know about this ...'

He pointed to the water meadows with his hickory. They were drifting into oblivion, their surfaces like black mirrors down below. A single heron was standing in the farthest corner like a grey sentry guarding the precious pastureland.

'I can do the master drowning. I were my father's apprentice for several years.'

Wickerman nodded thoughtfully.

'There seems to be more of you than I thought. What, did he have apprentices growing like grass around him? How many more of you, then, knows the skill? One, two, half-a-dozen?'

Tom shook his head.

'Only me.'

There was a growl in the throat of the heavens. Distant thunder was rapidly moving in. Wind started picking at the branches of the trees. It was dark enough now for the two figures on St Catherine's Hill to be hidden from local view.

'So, only one,' muttered Wickerman, moving to the boy's side.

'There's a storm coming,' said Tom, looking up. 'I saw lightning.'

'Where?' asked Wickerman. 'Point.'

Tom did as he was asked, lifting his arm and extending a finger.

While his arm was raised, Wickerman suddenly twisted the top of his hickory cane, and withdrew a sword.

'Ha!'

He plunged the blade into Tom's chest, at the side, under the armpit. It went in up to the gnarled knob of a hilt. It was the same method Wickerman had used to kill Angel Silke. He planned to take the boy's body and throw it into the river. When it was found, the wound would be nothing but a pinprick, a gnatbite, in a place where the finders would scarcely look. It would be believed that the boy had drowned.

Wickerman then stepped back after committing the act, withdrawing his rapier. At that moment sheet lightning flashed close to the hill.

Tom turned and looked at Wickerman with primal-black eyes. He gave no indication that he was in pain, nor did he drop to the ground as was expected. There was a terrible expression on his face, a look not natural to the living. There was nothing hostile, or violent in his stance. He simply poured grey contempt on his would-be murderer with those death-darkened eyes.

130

It was at that moment that Wickerman knew he was confronting a ghost.

'What's this!' cried the terrified man, dropping his sword stick. The blackness snapped shut around them as the thunder crashed over them in a great dry wave.

'Are you not mortal?' Wickerman whispered, unseeing.

No answer. The hired man stood there, trembling in the darkness, waiting to be engulfed by supernatural forces. His heart had turned to cold stone in his chest. He wanted to run, but all his energy had gone, drained from him into the Hampshire earth.

When the lightning flashed again, he saw he was alone.

Chapter Twenty-two

Somehow Wickerman found himself at The Green Man Inn. He went inside and sat in a corner, signalling to the landlady that he wanted some brandy. It was duly brought to him and the landlady made as if to speak, but Wickerman waved her away. He was in no mood for chat.

On lifting the pewter pot of brandy to his lips, Wickerman found he was still trembling violently. The drink spilled out of the sides of his mouth as his shivering hand rattled the pot against his teeth.

'Blast it,' he said to himself, 'I must be shaken up bad.'

He put the pot carefully on the wooden tabletop and then gripped his right hand in his left, in an attempt to control his nerves. Squeezing hard, so that it was painful and the fingers of his hand went white, he managed to concentrate on his condition and gradually to calm his thoughts. He knew he had received a great shock and he wanted to rationalise his experience.

It was a trick of the light, he thought. A storm can have that effect. In the grey dawn, or at evening twilight, a man begins to see things that are not really there. Just shadows, licking out of commonplace objects: a rock, or a tree. The mind plays tricks in such light, thinks it witnesses paranormal sights and sounds, but there were scientific explanations for such things. The mind is a conjurer.

Yet he heard the boy speak!

He took another gulp of his brandy, his shakes not so violent now that he was thinking things through. To occupy the mind, that was the important task.

He admitted to himself that he had always been afraid of the supernatural. Since he was a boy, when his grandmother had told him that the slate-faced phantom of his dead grandfather occupied an empty bed in the very same attic in which Wesley slept, he had been terrified of the dark hours.

He had never been able to confirm whether his grandmother's story was true or not, because once he was under the blanket he never dared look across the room at the other bed. He used to lie there and sweat, believing that the corpse of his grandfather was staring at him from a metre away. And the terror used to grow inside his head until he thought his skull would crack open with the pressure.

When you were afraid of something, he told himself, you thought about it too much. It became one of those things that went round and round in your brain, until you *made* some of it happen, in order to get it out of there. A kind of valve, that leaked your nightmares into the real world, in order to relieve the pressure.

He ordered another brandy.

That was it then. He had brought on this ghost of the master drowner's boy through having too much concern for the horrors of the night. If he thought about them just the same amount as any normal man, he would not be in distress.

By the time James Halliwell walked into the inn, flanked by two constables, Wickerman was once more the hard man, afraid of no one. The gypsy girl was also with the three men, her lurcher dog at her heels.

'Wickerman,' said James Halliwell, looking down on him, 'we have reason to believe you killed ...'

Wickerman started forward, clutching at his pot.

'Killed? Killed who?'

He thought of the boy on the hill. Had he been fooling himself after all? Maybe his mind had tricked him *after* the event, and the boy's body was there on the ground. He should have checked, instead of running away. He should have waited for a second lightning strike, and made sure the corpse was not actually lying in a pool of shadow, hidden from his gaze.

'... killed a man named Angel Silke,' finished Halliwell. 'Do you deny that you knew such a person?'

'He knowed him,' cried the girl Bess. 'I saw them together. Angel Silke and Wesley Wickerman. They was talking in here, and Meg and me came in as they was speaking.'

The two constables stood by, not saying anything, just watching Wickerman closely. They gripped their official clubs with farmer's-boy hands, calloused and soiled in the creases: hands more used to the holding of the plough than to bearing the badge of their office. They were yokels, for whom Wickerman felt nothing but contempt. Wickerman sensed that there was no direct proof available, or why would Halliwell be questioning him here, in a public inn?

'I don't know what you're talking about,' he said, leaning back in his chair and smiling at the stolid-looking constables. 'I haven't seen Angel since that night here, in the inn, after which I saw him on his way to London.'

Halliwell leaned over the table, his hands on the wooden surface, so that his eyes were only a few centimetres from Wickerman's.

'He never arrived in London. This note was opened by the landlady of his lodgings there, after he had been missing for six months. Apparently he was in the habit of leaving such letters, when he was working away from home.'

Halliwell straightened his back and unfolded a piece of paper, which he put down in front of Wickerman. The hired man did not move, but turned his eyes on the scrawl.

'TO MISES LUDGROVE, LANDLADY OF MY ADRESS. IF I FAILS TO COME BACK TO MY CHAMBERS CONSEQENT TO GOIN DOWN IN HAM-SHIRE COUNTY YOU MUST POINT THE LAW TOWARDS A PERSON WHAT GOES BY THE NAME OF WESLEY WICKERMAN. BE UNDER NO DOUBT HE HAS TURNED ME OFF FOR SOME REASONS OF HIS OWN. THE LAW MUST BE GAVE THIS NOTE UNDER CIRCUMSTANSES OF MY NOT RETURNIN. SIGNED ANGEL SILKE.'

'Chambers!' sneered Wickerman. 'He had a dirty little basement room, not big enough to turn around in.'

'Well, what to you say to it?' snapped Halliwell.

Wickerman flicked the note with the tips of his fingers, sending it down to the ale-sodden flags of the floor.

'What do I say to it? I say I wish Angel was here, to laugh along with me, I most sincerely do. He's probably having a good old grin at his joke, knowing fools like you would take him at his word. I wish he was here to see this. Instead he's probably sitting at some inn somewhere, telling those who'll listen what gullible people live in Hampshire, and how the constables in that county will come out for a member of the gentry whenever he whistles, like dogs called to heel by their master ...'

One of the constables started forward, but the other man restrained him.

'Leave it be, Jack,' said his friend. 'We'm here to arrest him, not be riled by 'un.'

Wickerman leaned back and cupped the back of his head in his hands.

'I suggest you take this gypsy and her cur and find yourself some evidence, *Mr* Halliwell, sir, before you come accusing honest men of terrible deeds of violence. Angel and me is good friends. I wish he was here to tell you hisself, but he seems to have gone somewhere he can't be reached. It's not the first time he's ducked out of lodgings, never to return. I'll wager my bootstraps he left owing some rent, eh? In debt, eh?'

He saw Halliwell's expression change, and he knew he had struck home. The only reason that old cow Ludgrove would bother taking Angel's note to the law would be because he left London owing her money, and she was hoping to be reimbursed by someone. Angel Silke had skipped more lodgings in his time than a travelling town mouse.

'Shall we arrest 'im, Mr Halliwell?' said one of the constables.

Halliwell stared for a long time at Wickerman's face, while

that man assumed an insolent expression in order to irritate his enemy.

Finally, Halliwell said, 'No, he's right. We have insufficient evidence. But we'll find some, eventually, and then it's the rope for you, Mr Wickerman, *sir*.'

With that, Halliwell turned and made for the door. One of the constables picked the note from the floor and then the pair of them followed, This left Bess and her lurcher Meg. Bess was looking at Wickerman with a half-smile on her smooth olive face. The dog's lean form was sitting, its head twisted round and up, regarding its mistress. It was ready to protect, should she give it a sign.

'Well?' snapped Wickerman, staring back at the gypsy girl with some distaste and not a little annoyance. 'What do you want?'

Bess's smile became wider, a haunting smile, as if she had scored some great victory which the vanquished party would not recognise, even though she was going to give him a clue as to why she knew she had won.

'You wished three times,' she said.

Chapter Twenty-three

James Halliwell left The Green Man Inn having accomplished what he set out to do, which was to arouse a feeling of unease and insecurity in Wesley Wickerman. James knew there was not enough evidence on which they could arrest the hired man, but he had wanted to put Wickerman on the defensive. It was time to bring Sir Francis Alderton's sins home to roost.

The note from Mrs Ludgrove was genuine enough, and James was fairly certain that something sordid had befallen Angel Silke. Whether Wickerman had actually harmed the missing man remained to be discovered, but it was not uncommon for cut-throats like Wickerman and Silke to fall out and to turn their ugly talents against each other.

What interested James more was the fact that something had been bothering Wickerman, even before that man had spotted James and the two constables. James spoke about this with Alex and Jem Blunden.

'He was ill at ease, and had clearly been shaken quite badly. He was pale, perspiring profusely, his movements were jerky and nervous, and he was drinking, not for enjoyment, but the way a man drinks when he's assailed by some fear. I'm trying to think what it could be to cause him such anguish.'

Jem said, 'Maybe Sir Francis?'

Alex Blunden shook his head.

'No, son. He bain't afeared of Sir Francis.'

'I'm inclined to agree with your father, Jem. It goes deeper than that. Some irrational fear had been touched. Are you afraid of large spiders, Jem?'

Jem nodded, seemingly reluctant.

'Not fond of 'em.'

'It's *that* kind of fear I'm talking about. Something deeply rooted in the soul, and quite absurd ...'

'I don't think it's absurd to be afeared of spiders,' replied Jem quickly. James guessed Jem was protecting his manhood.

'Oh, make no mistake, Jem, I'm scared of spiders myself. Especially the large hairy kind you find in the barn straw. I remember screaming blue murder as a boy, when one as big as your hand crawled up my shirt, as I was tumbling with my brother in the hay sheaves ...'

Both Jem and his father shuddered.

'... but in all truth, spiders in England are not harmful. There's no real reason why we should be so terrified of them. It's just one of these deep-seated fears that goes back to Adam. Snakes, spiders – anyway, this is getting us nowhere. What I'm trying to say is that Wickerman has been frightened by something like that, and if we can find out what it is, we can make use of it.'

They talked some more, but came to the sad conclusion that they were no nearer to trapping Wickerman than they had been at the beginning of the evening, when James had heard that Mrs Ludgrove's note was in the possession of the local Anglican priest, the Reverend Timothy Withstanding, through whom all correspondence addressed 'to whom it may concern' was filtered. James had called upon the vicar and the Reverend had left the matter with him to pursue.

The meeting broke up shortly afterwards and James rode home on Sheba.

Chapter Twenty-four

While the meeting between James Halliwell and the two Blundens was in progress, Wickerman had a visitor of his own. He was supping his sixth brandy when a coach arrived at the inn and someone of rank entered the house from the rear and took a private room. A few minutes later a maid came and whispered to Wickerman that Sir Francis Alderton was wished to see him. Lighted candle in hand, the maid then led the way up a narrow winding staircase, to a room in the east wing of the inn.

Wickerman was ushered into the great man's presence by a valet.

Sir Francis was not in a good mood.

He looked up at Wickerman from beneath his bushy greying eyebrows and growled, 'Well, what's this I hear? Those tenant farmers have put one over on you? What? Speak up, man.'

'They seem to have found someone to do the drowning for 'em, but I've got plans to stop all that.'

Sir Francis grunted.

'I don't want to hear about any *plans*. I want to see those water meadows in a useless condition, do you hear me? For years now I've allowed myself to be patient with these people. I can be so no longer. We have to destroy their system.'

Wickerman nodded, vigorously.

'That's what I was thinking. We need to find this Master Drowner and ...'

Sir Francis waved an impatient hand at him, as if he were brushing away an annoying insect.

'Never mind *finding* anyone. I want you to blow the damn thing up. I want the main sluice to be matchwood before tomorrow morning, do you understand me? Have you any gunpowder? You'll need at least two casks.'

Wickerman's mind was spinning. An explosion? How would he manage that? And was it a wise thing for him to be doing, directly after being accused of murder? Things seemed to be getting a little out of his control.

'I have the powder, back at the cottage, but I won't do it,' he said, flatly.

The aristocrat, who had been staring at the wall, awaiting an answer, also exploded himself.

'Won't do it? Won't? *Won't?*'

'That is,' said Wickerman, hastily revising his emphatic statement, 'I can't do it – not unless you pays me a large sum, and then let's me go on my way. I'm marked in this place now. I can't stay around here forever, with everybody hating me. Someone's bound to have a go at me soon. They'll trump up some sort o' charge against me, and frankly, sir, I don't trust you to intervene and save me.'

There was a snort from the other man.

'Running away, eh? You, Wickerman?'

'Temporary, just temporary. Well, what about it, sir? A nice big bag of billies and I'll blow that sluice into the clouds. It'll be raining splinters for a week afterwards. Then it won't matter how many master drowners they get themselves. The season'll be ruined, and you'll be able to buy the mortgages from the banks.'

'Billies?' murmured the aristocrat, in a half-amused tone.

'Gold coins. You know what I mean.'

Sir Francis began to pace the room, his heels clicking on the bare boards of the floor. There was the smell of final victory in the air. It was so very close.

Wickerman said, sensing the baronet's thoughts, 'Shame to let it all go now, just for the sake of a few billies, sir.'

'All right,' said Sir Francis. 'You shall have your "billies" and a night passage to France. How does that suit you? Once the job has been completed, make your way down to Southampton water. Ask for a sea captain called Courtney. The name of his ship is the *Sea Eagle*. In the meantime, I shall send a courier with a message. My man will get there before you, since you have work to do, and see that you make the morning tide.'

Wickerman said, 'If he's not there, with the money, you know what'll happen, of course?'

Sir Francis winced.

'I don't like threats, Wickerman. The money and the passage will be waiting. Please don't bore me with a display of your backstreet culture. Just do the job. Good night.'

'Good night and goodbye, sir.'

With that Sir Francis signalled for him to leave the room.

Wickerman went down to the parlour and ordered another pot of brandy. He needed it to give his courage a bolster. While he was supping it, he heard the clatter of hooves on the courtyard cobbles, and knew that Alderton's coach was on its way back to the baronet's house.

The hired man began to feel pleasantly warm inside. It had been an evening of many events. He had been accosted by a phantom – oh, yes, he could admit that to himself now – and accused of murdering his comrade. These were unpleasant and undesirable happenings, which he hoped to put behind him.

France? He didn't know any French, but Calais was full of English-speaking families. Merchants mostly. He'd find something to do, especially with a bag full of billies. Open his own trading house, perhaps? Buy into something good, something with a bit of flare. A smuggler's boat, maybe? Have some other fool run the risks for a change? It all sounded very promising.

Yes, he would blow up the main sluice, but he wanted someone on the flood plain when he did so. He smiled into his brandy. Halliwell. He would get that young squire's whelp and drown him at the same time as putting the farmers out of business. The force of the water from the Itchen, when he blew the sluice, would sweep away anyone in its path.

Wickerman imagined himself on the deck of the *Sea Eagle*,

the salt spray on his face as he looked back toward England, knowing that there was a corpse washing around the water meadows.

Mr James Halliwell.

The man was going to die.

Chapter Twenty-five

James found himself being woken at half-past two by one of his servants informing him that there was a man downstairs by the name of Sam Teppit, with a message for him.

He rose and put something over his nightshirt before descending the stairs and finding the lock-keeper's assistant waiting for him, cap in hand. The man handed James a note.

'I brought you this, sir. Mr Wickerman said to give it to nobody but you, an' that's what I done.'

Teppit shuffled his feet around awkwardly.

James said, 'Thank you,' very coldly. He read the note, which asked him to be at a certain place on the water meadows at precisely four o'clock that morning 'to settle accounts between us'. The message was signed 'Wesley Wickerman'.

So, Wickerman had not suggested a duel, which he must know would have been out of the question anyway. Duels are fought between gentlemen of near-equal rank, not between squire's sons and street fighters. What he had sent was simply a challenge, a test of James Halliwell's courage.

James could of course ignore the message, and still not feel that his honour had been dented. It was certain that Wickerman was a felon, most likely a murderer. One did not need to prove oneself against such men.

Still, James decided, there was nothing he could do, at the moment, which would put Wickerman behind bars. Perhaps it was the only solution, to meet this thug out in the open, and 'settle accounts' between them.

James stared at Sam Teppit.

'Tell your master,' he said after a while, 'that I shall be glad to accommodate him.'

Sam's usual damp expression suddenly showed a few sparks glowing beneath its wet ashen surface. He drew himself up before saying, 'I wouldn't call him my *master*, sir. I don't think he's that. I just work the lock for him.'

There was something in the way that Sam Teppit had come back so swiftly which caused James to believe he had touched a raw nerve.

'You don't like Mr Wickerman?'

'I hates him!' said Sam Teppit, vehemently.

There was silence between them.

Then Sam Teppit obviously thought some sort of explanation was required.

'I didn't know the man, afore I come down to Hampshire to work the lock, but I were desperate for employment and most likely would have come anyways, whatever he were like. He's the Devil, though, sir, or one of his minions. He treats me worse'n a dog, and that's a fact. I know it's a terrible thing to say, but I shouldn't care if he fell in the river after drinkin' his way through a barrel and drowned away.'

James smiled at Sam's obvious discomfort with the thought that he desired harm to befall a man. Sam was incapable of violence himself, and the only way he could retaliate against such a bully as Wickerman was to call on natural justice to intervene on his behalf.

'Perhaps Mr Wickerman will not be with us much longer, Sam. I have heard he is going away soon, and might not return in our lifetimes.'

Hope sprang to the eyes of Sam Teppit.

'Oh, I do wish it. I do wish it heartily,' said the lock-keeper's assistant.

Once Sam had gone on his way, with the acknowledgement, James took a brace of duelling pistols from a cabinet in the library and proceeded to clean and load the weapons. He was a poor shot, with any kind of firearm, but these two pistols were finely made by one of the best gunsmiths in Britain. If he had to arm himself, he could not do better than his brother's set of balanced duelling pistols.

Loaded and primed, he took them upstairs to his bedroom,

144

where he dressed. He stuck the hand guns into the waistband of his riding breeches. Then he stood in front of the mirror and admired himself.

'Very rakish,' he murmured. 'I would frighten myself if I met me on the highway.'

He decided to take with him some spare kerchiefs, to use as bandages if necessary, and searched the top drawer of his dressing table. There he found what he was looking for, and something else besides. It was a half-finished poem dedicated to a Miss Edwina Caudieron, begun some few years ago. She was now of course Mrs Halliwell, the wife of his dear brother, and he took the poem and set a match to it. He watched the sonnet burn in a small Chinese dish decorated with cranes and cherry blossoms. The flame, James decided, was quite exotic, considering it was an ordinary piece of paper. Perhaps the verses on it made it burn with such brilliance and colour?

He considered how fortunate he was that Nellie, the maid who was supposed to look after his wardrobe, did not exert herself in her search for duties to perform. Had she found this scrap of manuscript, a remnant of his romantic youth when he was ready to die (on paper anyway) for love, he would have been the talk of the servants' quarters.

He amused himself with certain tasks, careful not to make a noise and rouse either his father or his brother and his wife, until the time came to leave for the water meadows.

Chapter Twenty-six

Once Sam Teppit had been sent on his errand, Wickerman went to his bedroom and drew a chest out from beneath the brewer's-dray bed. Inside the trunk there were several small drawers and from one of these he took a padlock key. Armed with this piece of metal and a lamp, he went outside the cottage to a shed standing in some trees, some twenty metres' distance from the lock. He opened the rusted lock with a little difficulty and went inside the shed.

He emerged a few minutes later with two small but heavy barrels, one under each arm, and took the river path to the water meadows. The lamp he held between his teeth, and it swung to and fro, making him grunt occasionally.

There was a moon of sorts, like a hook hanging from the night, being bothered by some skittish clouds. Some stars were out, faint and misty-lighted, as if viewed from the bottom of a pond. It was chill, but not freezing, and there was a kind of awakedness about the banks of the river and the fields beyond, as if the creatures there were up and about, doing certain daytime tasks while the rest of the world slept.

When Wickerman reached the main sluice, attached to a short spur of the Itchen itself, he rested the barrels on the ground. The lamp he put on the bank by the sluice. From his inside pocket he took some baling string, and finding it a bit too short for his purposes, took the string from around his trouser bottoms and joined all three pieces together. With this he tied the barrels to the posts in the middle of the sluice, at the join between the gates where it was at its weakest.

He surveyed his work with satisfaction.

Then he turned and looked down on the flood plain, where thousands of litres of water would flow, once the sluice had been breached. The land there was over four metres lower than the river and the torrents of water that would come gushing through the gap would sweep any mortal off his feet and rush him to a breathless end.

Wickerman then made his way back to the cottage. In his room was a long sporting gun. Although he could not use pistols with any accuracy, which is why he had not taken Halliwell up on his ch llenge that time at the inn, he was proficient with a rifle.

Wickerman had not fought against the French, like many of the drowners, and would have considered such profitless action to be a worthless duty. Wickerman had seen the wounded and maimed on the streets of London after the wars. He had witnessed them being harassed by the law. In fact, rather than fund hospitals for the soldiers who had come home from the continent with missing limbs and disease-ravaged bodies, Parliament had passed a bill stating that anyone found begging on the streets could be thrown into jail. If that was the thanks the populace got for fighting for their country, Wickerman wanted none of it.

No, his shooting skills had been learned in Suffolk, where he had spent some years with a poacher friend after finding Tilbury too hot for him at the time. He could hit a hare on the run with remarkable ease. *Had* he been a soldier, he would have been the pride of the regiment, having all the necessary skills for battle: a marksman with a rifle, deadly with a blade, and good with his fists and feet. Wickerman was a man born to violence, be it art or science.

He sat at a small table and cleaned and primed the weapon, much as James Halliwell was doing with his pistols at that present moment. Once, when he was using the pull-through to lightly oil the inside of the barrel, he thought he saw a shadow move by his bed.

He started, and turned quickly to look, but there was nothing there and he decided that the lamp must have guttered.

Later, when he was preparing to leave, he was sure he felt a presence in the room behind him. This time he did not turn round, but made purposefully for the doorway, his heart thumping against his ribcage.

'I'm not going to play to such fanciful thoughts,' he told himself. 'It's because I'm out on the murder that I keep thinking someone's watching me. It's my guilty conscience, and I won't pay heed to it. I've done too many to death now, to be saved by repentance, and I won't listen ...'

He took the river path again, to the sluice gates.

There were soft sounds amongst the tree tops, as if things were caught in the tangle of the branches, like shadows with substance.

Birds, thought Wickerman. *Just birds.*

There were night moves which had no accountable reason behind them, but Wickerman rationalised each small sight or sound. A dark shape flying across the river was an owl or bat: a rustling in the grasses were the stirrings of harmless creatures in sleep.

A cold wind came from nowhere, like the blast from a supernatural place, and halted him in his tracks. He had heard that such frozen gusts were common at the funeral of a witch, and looked upwards to see a single strangely-shaped cloud moving sombrely overhead.

'I'll not be bothered by this,' he told himself. 'Imagination and fancy, that's all it is. I can do my work at night, as well as in the day. The sun's gone down, the light's been took, and that's all. Nothing more to it.'

He stopped short of the main sluice by about twenty metres. He remained on high ground, amongst some gorse bushes on the river bank, where he could see the barrels of gunpowder on the wooden barriers.

At four o'clock there was enough light in the sky to aim by. Wickerman sighted along the barrel. He knew he could not miss at this range. The farmers were going to lose their meadows after all, despite having been helped by a ghost.

Wickerman shivered, as he remembered.

Tom Timbrell.

The boy's phantom had given him a great fright, that much was sure, but when he had heard the boys talking, Tom Timbrell had said he was going away, *had* to go away, and therefore would not be around to haunt his enemies.

In any case, a malevolent spirit could only cause harm to the person responsible for its death.

Wickerman was sure of that because the gypsies (who knew about such things) had told him as much.

He sighted down the barrel again.

A half-heard dialogue came back into his mind now. He had not listened or been able to hear the whole of the conversation that had gone on between Jem Blunden and Tom Timbrell, but bits of it had floated to him in his hiding place on St Catherine's Hill when they had taken their parting. Now that he had the silence of the night around him, and time to contemplate, he considered what he had heard for the first time since the eavesdropping.

Something about a dead person. A corpse. Something about its spirit not finding a home. What? It had to be found and taken care of ...? That was it – if the corpse was lost to the world the spirit was trapped between earth and heaven. It was doomed to wander in the nether world of night, until its body was found and put in the earth.

A figure appeared on the flood plain below. It was Halliwell, walking up towards the main sluice.

That was why Tom Timbrell had been promised by Jem Blunden that his body would be found. It was lost somewhere, at the bottom of the Itchen, and his soul was abroad.

'He can't hurt me,' muttered Wickerman, 'I never did the boy no harm.'

He said this, yet he sensed something awful in the night around him, as if the dawn were bringing in some foul thing which the world would be better without. A voice inside him told him to run, to go away, far away, but he was a stubborn man and though he might have given up demolishing the sluice, he could not go without killing Halliwell.

He lined up the sights and found his target, the two barrels of gunpowder. When he pulled the trigger the hot bullet would be sent on its way to ignite the powder.

Halliwell was not far below the sluice now, looking round him, as if he expected an ambush. Well, he was going to get one, but not from any considered quarter. He was going to be swept off his feet and taken to his doom.

Again, that terrible feeling of foreboding washed through the murderer. He tried to ignore it, telling himself it was just his stupid conscience trying to turn him away from his plan to destroy his enemy.

'Only a phantom what has been harmed by me, can harm me back,' murmured Wickerman, his finger tightening on the trigger. 'I can't be touched by the boy. The boy has gone back to his water-grave, wherever that lies.'

Halliwell was now in the right spot.

Wickerman drew a deep breath, steadied his arm, and began squeezing the trigger ...

Just at that moment, there was a no-sound behind him. It was a noise, but not a noise. It was just ... something. The fine hairs on Wickerman's neck raised themselves, as if he had been touched by static in a lightning storm. A quivering went through his body as his senses became finely tuned, to the point of being painful: a kind of prickling, stinging sensation that almost robbed him of breath.

Slowly, Wesley Wickerman turned, and his brain jangled in his skull at what he saw. His breath came out in sharp grunts and his teeth clattered together.

There was a figure, a man, standing just a metre away, looking down on him. The creature had on raggedy clothes, which smelled of old earth, and a dirty kerchief was knotted at its throat. Its features were thoroughly familiar to Wickerman – a face like a hatchet and matted black hair that hung down to a filthy collar – and it wore an ashen, humourless smile.

The figure spoke in hollow accents.

'Hello, Wes,' said Angel Silke, 'I've come to do you a bit of mischief.'

Wickerman's heart was full of fear, pumping horror around his body, through every vein and artery. It stilled every other thought within his head. Only terror remained there: a dread that sent red mist before his eyes. His ears heard a shrill scream coming from somewhere close by, not knowing that the sound came from his own lips.

'Oh, God,' he groaned, then he pointed his weapon and pulled the trigger.

The gun roared, the shot tearing the belly out of the night.

'Wes,' Silke cried, the ball having passed through him without any apparent wound, 'is that any greeting for an old pal? Here, give Angel your hand ...'

Chapter Twenty-seven

'When I reached the river bank,' said James to the group before him, 'Wickerman was on his knees, his face pressed down into the grasses. His discharged weapon was lying at his side. God knows what he had fired at, but it wasn't me, nor was it the casks of powder tied to the sluice.

'Anyway, he insisted he show me where the body of Angel Silke lay, right at that moment. We collected two constables and went out to an old shepherd's hut, on the downs ...'

'I know that place,' Jem gasped. 'I been there.'

The youth clutched for Bess's hand and, on finding it, squeezed it hard.

'... anyway, there was a disused well close by, and an investigation of its depths revealed two rotten corpses, that of a sheep — and that of Angel Silke. Wickerman confessed to having murdered the man. He also implicated Sir Francis Alderton in the plot to blow up the sluice. Sir Francis, as you all know, is now somewhere in France, having escaped the troopers that were sent to apprehend him.'

'We'll get 'im,' growled Whoffer Riley. ''Ee won't show his nose around here for some whiles, and when 'ee do, oi'll be a waitin'. Oi'll drag him off to the jailhouse where 'ee'll spend a bit o' time, I'll put my stump on it.'

The rest of the group, which consisted of most of the drowners, Bess and Meg, and Mrs Blunden, were not so sure. They knew that the gentry had ways of getting round the law, but at least Sir Francis was out of their hair for the time being and, who knew, he might like it in France and stay there until his death caught up with him?

'What about Martha Timbrell?' asked Jem. 'Will she be coming back?'

James Halliwell shook his head.

152

'I think not, Jem. The family are well settled in Norfolk now. But the authorities have appointed Sam Teppit to the position of lock-keeper – he's been doing the job for a year or so now, after all – and he's very pleased to be there.'

'I'm sure he is,' growled Alex Blunden.

'Now, Blunden, some charity if you please,' said his wife. 'Sam Teppit were not Wickerman's animal. He were caught up in something not of his doing, as Mr Halliwell told us.'

The rest of the group agreed with this.

'So,' finished James, 'all in all we've been very fortunate. Things have worked out for the good and now I have work to do. We have to find Tom Timbrell's present resting place and put him where he belongs ...'

They found Tom's body, snagged on the brickwork beneath the arch of a mill, down past Twyford. His remains were duly transported to the graveyard, where they were buried alongside his father John.

Jem was both relieved and pleased that he had been able to do this service for his old enemy, and later, friend.

Sometimes, very occasionally, on summer days when the tics were jumping in the straw, and the world was too hot a place for physical activity, Jem would go to the graveside and pass a few words with Tom, telling him how things were coming along in the world of the living.

Tom never answered, of course, but Jem knew that his words would find their way to the Master Drowner's apprentice, wherever he was between earth, river and sky. Jem knew it because he felt it, and when there are no other signposts, one's emotions are the surest guides to the truth.